Locket's Meadow

Ozzie's Promise

Written and Illustrated by

Kathleen M. Schurman

authorHOUSE®

AuthorHouse™
1663 Liberty Drive
Bloomington, IN 47403
www.authorhouse.com
Phone: 1 (800) 839-8640

Published by AuthorHouse 03/06/2017

ISBN: 978-1-5246-7053-5 (sc)
ISBN: 978-1-5246-7420-5 (e)

Print information available on the last page.

This book is printed on acid-free paper.

For Falstaff, Ozzie Osboar, Ragano, Classy and all those animals whose love has touched and forever changed my heart. The day we collectively crash that Rainbow Bridge will become a legend often retold across the Universes, and always with a smile.

Ozzie's Promise
Prologue
The Terrible, Terrifying Miracle
June 2008, Des Moines County Iowa

Rain. Endless rain. The sound of rain pounding on the metal roof high above them droned on for days, lulling the hundreds of pigs beneath it into a melancholy trance.

"Sister," said Harriet as she slowly lifted herself to her feet, her belly heavy with babies. "I hear The Men say it is 'rain' that hits the roof above us, but what, I wonder, does that mean?"

"Not a hill of beans, Sister," said Ice, peering at her through her blue eye, which was the left one, as her neck was too stiff to turn and look at her through her brown one, as well.

Ice also decided to haul herself to her feet. Standing gave her some relief from lying in the slime of her own manure and urine, yet once she lifted her own heavy belly off the floor, she felt the familiar ache in her legs and wondered . . . what was the point? Standing, sitting, lying down . . . it was all the same. Neither she nor her sister had left their crates for more than a few minutes at a time since they'd been put into them, and that had been several years earlier.

There were hundreds of sows in the enormous barn and each of their bodies filled their crates so completely that none of them could move an inch.

Ice opened her mouth and clenched a bar of her gate in her teeth. If she bit down hard enough she sometimes forgot about the aches in her body.

"Sister," Harriet said, "I have told you that you will ruin your teeth doing that!"

"Oh, for goodness sake," Ice snapped. "What difference would it make?"

She bit back down on the bar, then opened her mouth and tried, as she often did, to stretch her tongue far enough to reach the latch on the gate. If only she could push it up and over she knew she could shove the door open and let herself out, then maybe take a slow stroll down the aisle to help relieve the pain in her stiff body. She opened her mouth wide and pushed her snout as close to the latch as she could, but as always, failed.

"Sister, if only I could get my teeth around it," she said, "I know I could get it open."

"But you can't, my dear," Harriet patiently replied, lying back down on the hard floor and feeling the familiar burn of the slime on the skin of her belly.

At the far end of the aisle, over the noise of the pounding rain, the pair of lady pigs heard a commotion. They turned their heads and strained to see through the dim light.

"What is it, Sister?" Harriet asked, again rising to her feet. "Can you see?"

Ice stared down the aisle, trying to hear what the other sows were shouting about. And then . . . she saw . . . and gasped. "It's water," she cried. "Look at the floor . . . Look towards the door . . . there is water coming into the barn!"

The large doors at the opposite end of the barn slid open with a whoosh and a clang and The Men rushed inside.

"The water overtopped the sandbags!" one of then shouted. "Let the pigs out or they'll drown!"

"But there's no place to put 'em!" another one shouted. "Everything is flooding!"

"We're going to lose everything . . . everything!" shouted another.

Harriet and Ice looked back towards the other end of the barn, and what had been a thin sheet of water sliding towards them across the cement was now a low, rippling wall.

Terrified, Ice clenched the bar of her crate and screamed at the top of her lungs, but over the noise of the rain crashing against the roof, the other screaming pigs and the shouting of the men, no one noticed.

The Men began to open crates, flinging aside gates and quickly moving on, and the freed sows clambered out into the aisle, but with so much chaos, they had no idea where to go. The water had already reached the ladies and in a matter of a minute was up to their knees. Ice clenched the metal bar in her teeth and screamed again, but Harriet, who seldom shouted, screamed right over the top of her.

"Sister, Sister!" she shouted. "They are almost here! The Men are almost here!"

One of them had sloshed through the water and was a few crates away, and the ladies heard him curse as he fought his way through a sea of screaming pigs, slipping and sliding his way up the aisle. The water lapped against the pigs' bellies as he reached to unlatch Harriet's gate and set her free, but another huge sow, not knowing which way to turn, knocked him to his knees. He struggled back to his feet, but instead of opening Harriet's door, skipped past and opened Ice's.

The water was at her shoulder as she shoved past the gate and into the aisle

"Run Sister!" Harriet shouted. "Run!!!!"

The Man continued past them and up the aisle, leaving Harriet trapped behind a locked gate.

Ice braced herself against the rushing water and the crush of pigs flailing about in the dim light.

"Run!" Harriet shouted again. "Get out!!!"

Sow after sow pressed up against Ice in a desperate frenzy to save themselves, but Ice clenched her teeth onto one of the bars of

Harriet's gate and held on tightly, waiting for a moment when no one was slamming into her. And then, with the water lapping at her chin, she let go, grabbed the latch and, just as she had imagined doing a thousand times over, lifted it high and slid it to the side.

"Push!" Ice shouted. "Push it open!"

Harriet shoved her head against her prison door. It swung open into the rushing water and she staggered into the aisle.

"Now what do we do?" she cried. "Things are looking grim!"

"Dearest Sister, we will swim!" Ice yelled back. "Swim as hard as you can! And we mustn't lose sight of each other!"

Mama and Ozzie Osboar

Chapter One

This Little Piggy
Mid August, Bethany, Connecticut

David tossed one last bale of hay through the haymow door and into the bed of the blue pickup truck below. He wiped the sweat from his forehead with the sleeve of his T-shirt, leaned against the open mow door and looked out over the horse paddock where Beatrice, Benny, Bingo and Bart were dozing. It was late in the afternoon, but the August sun burned down onto the farm, baking the earth and slowing all living beings to a crawl. Even the bees humming above the butterfly bushes lingered longer than usual as they burrowed into each purple blossom, resting a few moments before moving on to the next one.

As he turned to climb down the stairs to the barn aisle, David's cell phone rang and he took a moment to wipe the sweat from his ear before answering it.

"Hello?"

"Hey, Dave, it's Richie."

Richie was the man who delivered hay to the farm every month.

"Now Dave, I'm calling you instead of Kathleen so you can say no if you want," Richie said. "You don't have to do this."

"Do what?" David asked.

"Well, you know we raise pigs, and two days ago we had a runt born," he said. "My daughter's trying to keep it alive with a bottle and he's not doing well, and we've never managed to keep a runt alive before, they're real difficult, but there's something about this one . . . I don't know what it is . . ."

"A pig, huh?" David said.

"Now I don't want you to feel any pressure," Richie said. "You can say no and we can pretend we never had this conversation. Kathleen doesn't have to know anything."

David sat down on a bale of hay.

"Richie, do you know my wife?" David said.

"Well, yes, but . . ."

"If we didn't say anything at all," David said, "she'd still figure it out. Once it's out of your mouth it's already too late. Sometimes even before that."

"I want you to know, he's a very sick little pig," Richie said. "His chances aren't good."

"If anyone can save him, it's Kathleen," David said, and hung up the phone to go find his wife.

There were two driveways to enter the farm. One led past the little cottage where David and Kathleen's daughter Bo lived with her husband Craig. It continued on past the big horse barn, where David had been throwing hay bales, and the indoor horseback riding arena.

Then it curved up the hill between the many horse paddocks. The driveway next door to it on Old Litchfield Turnpike was where he and Kathleen lived in a little white house next to a little white barn. David drove out one side of the farm and back in on the other driveway. He left the hay on the truck and walked up the slate sidewalk, stomped his dirty boots clean, then entered the house.

The kitchen was heavy with the scent of fresh tomatoes. The heat of August always brought ripe tomatoes from the garden, hundreds more than they could eat, so Kathleen made them into huge pots of sauce to preserve in glass jars for meals throughout the winter.

"Hey Baby," she said as her husband walked in. She always called him Baby unless she was angry with him, and then she called him David. Ragano, the brown farm dog who looked like a coyote and always stayed at Kathleen's feet, lifted his head and glanced at David, then tucked his nose back beneath the tip of his bushy tail. Agnes, the little Jack Rat Terrier, trotted over and sniffed his boots and David reached way down and gave her a pat. She was no bigger than any of the kitchen cats, and was almost all white except for a few brown spots.

"Can you grab one more basket of tomatoes from the mudroom for me?" Kathleen asked.

"Got it," he said, and stepped out through the kitchen door to fetch one.

"Thanks," Kathleen said as David set it on the kitchen table.

"Um . . . Richie called," David said, picking a perfectly ripe tomato from the basket.

"Do we need more hay already?"

"No, no," David said, and he rinsed the tomato in the sink and took a bite – it was still warm from the hot summer sun. "He asked if we wanted a little runt pig he's got over there."

"A runt pig?"

"I guess it's sick," he said.

"We've never had a pig," Kathleen said. A long strand of curly, blonde hair had fallen out of her ponytail and she tucked it behind her ear. "I'm not sure what to do with one."

"Well, Richie doesn't seem to think this one's going to make it, he's pretty sick, but I said I'd ask you about him."

"Not going to make it?" Kathleen said. "Oh, boy. I don't know. I've never even thought about having a pig. Poor little thing. You know what? It can't hurt to try. Call Richie back and tell him we'll take it."

David smiled. He'd already known she couldn't turn away a sick animal. Before he could pick up his cell phone to return Richie's call Kathleen had already retrieved her laptop computer, set it on the counter next to a row of canning jars and typed "raising piglets" into the search engine.

Two hours later Richie arrived at the kitchen door. Kathleen rushed to let him in, not really knowing what to expect. She'd seen piglets at the Durham Fair, all piled up with their mamas under heat lamps, but she had no idea how small a runt piglet would be. When Richie reached out to hand her the tiny animal, she was shocked – it was no bigger than a guinea pig.

Kathleen gently took the baby in her hands, sat in a kitchen chair, and held him up to her eyes.

"Look at you, you sweet angel!" she murmured. "How perfect are you!"

The tiny piglet looked her right in the eye, broke out in a huge grin and gave a squeal of delight. Ragano placed his feet on Kathleen's thighs and began to clean the piglet's ears, which is what he always did when there was a new baby on the farm. Agnes danced around, leaping high into the air trying to get a better look.

"Just wait, puppies," Kathleen said. "You can play with him when he's feeling better. Oh, I love him!" she said, nuzzling her nose to his snout. He was no bigger than her cupped hands and perfectly pale pink all over. "David, can you run to the garage and get the old guinea pig cage and put some pine shavings in it? This baby is going to live on the kitchen table for now."

"That was easy," Richie said.

"Yeah, well, it usually is," David sighed.

It had been eight years since the couple moved to their farm in Bethany, Connecticut and named it Locket's Meadow after their very special burro, Locket, who had been rescued years earlier from the scorching deserts of Death Valley. From the very beginning they had saved all kinds of farm animals from some very scary places. Many horses had come and stayed, while many, many more had been rescued and adopted out to other safe homes. Along with the horses and Locket there were dozens of other animals, including chickens, goats, ducks and more . . . but there had never been a pig on the farm.

"What are you feeding him?" Kathleen asked. "And what's wrong with him?"

Richie explained they were feeding him bottles of evaporated milk, and that he had developed terrible diarrhea from it. Kathleen nodded and said nothing, but she scurried around the kitchen collecting up milk replacer powder and baby bottles. She'd spent the past few hours reading up on piglets between processing jars of tomatoes, and she now knew what to do.

"Thanks so much for taking him," Richie said. "We have hundreds and hundreds of pigs born every year, but I dunno . . . there's just something about this one. Something . . . I dunno," he said and scratched his head.

Richie said his goodbyes, and David placed the cage on the island in the kitchen. Word had gotten around the farm that there was a new arrival, and people began to stop by to visit him. Bo and Craig had heard the news and were the first to arrive, walking over from their little cottage next door. They got there just as Kathleen had settled onto a kitchen chair with the new baby and a warm bottle of milk.

"Oh, Mom! He's so tiny!" Bo exclaimed as she bent over the piglet, who was quickly draining his bottle. "What are you going to name him?"

"I don't know," Kathleen said. "I haven't even thought about it yet . . . but . . ."

"But?" Bo repeated.

"Well, don't think I'm crazy, but . . . when Richie handed him to me and he looked right into my eyes, I could have sworn I heard him say . . ."

"What?" Bo asked.

"I swear, I heard him say, 'I'm a rock star!'"

Bo burst out laughing. "Of course he is! Just look at him!"

"But then, he needs a rock star name, don't you think?" Kathleen said.

It was Craig's turn to burst out laughing. "This is an easy one!" he said. "What about Ozzie!"

Kathleen smiled. "You mean . . . Ozzie Os*boar*?"

And the tiny piglet let go of his bottle, looked up at his new mother, and gave a happy squeal.

"Ozzie Osboar, it is," Kathleen said. "I guess we have ourselves a real rock star on the farm."

The entire house was dark and quiet when Ragano nudged Agnes awake. By the light of the moon shining in through the skylights of the old farmhouse, the pair silently slid off the bed. Ragano led the way across the floor, stood on his hind legs, then used his right front paw to lower the handle and push open one of the French doors. Then they slipped down the narrow stairs, through the hallway and into the kitchen.

"What is it?" Agnes asked Ragano for the one-hundredth time.

"I don't know!" the bigger, older dog replied. "They keep saying it's a pig, but I've never seen a pig before, so I have no idea."

The guinea pig cage sat on the antique farm table in the center of the kitchen and Ragano stood on his hind legs, set his paws on the edge of the table and peered at the tiny, pink creature snuggled into the pine shavings beneath a heat lamp that at one time had been used to keep an iguana warm.

"Nope," Ragano said. "I've never seen anything like this before."

Ragano had lived on the farm for three years, ever since Kathleen adopted him from the Milford Animal Shelter. He'd heard the story told many times of how she'd found him. The animal control officer, Rick George, had called Kathleen one late November day.

"Hey, Kathleen," Rick said. "I don't know if you're in the market for another dog, but I have one here at the pound and every time I look at him I hear your name."

"Oh, boy," Kathleen replied. "I don't know . . . but tell me about him."

"He was born here about four weeks ago," Rick said. "And I've been thinking I need to call you for, oh, about four weeks, now."

"You know, I won't call David just yet," she said, "but I'll meet you at the shelter in about twenty-five minutes."

Kathleen had climbed into the big, blue farm truck and driven straight to the animal shelter, and Rick led her into the kennels and stopped in front of a thin, black mama dog who was nursing a huge, wiggling pile of puppies . . . all of them coal black except for one.

Kathleen burst out laughing. "It's that fat, fluffy brown one you're thinking of, isn't it?"

"Well," Rick said. "You decide for yourself."

She knelt on the floor and cracked open the kennel. She'd decided the best thing to do was to take them out one at a time and see how they reacted to her, ending with the brown puppy. After many years of rescuing animals she'd learned that the one who comes home with you isn't always the one you think it's going to be. So she scooped up one of the chubby black ones and set it on her lap. The puppy was very friendly and snuggly, but not exactly "the one," and when Kathleen set her back in the kennel she waddled back to her mother. The next black one did the same, as did puppy number three and all the way up to puppy number seven.

Puppy number eight was the roly-poly little brown one, who had parked himself at the gate and stared at her while she visited with the others. Kathleen reached in and lifted him up to eye level, and the little dog lunged toward her, wrapped his paws around her neck and wouldn't let go.

"Uh, Rick? Does he usually do this?" she asked.

"Nope," he replied. "Never seen him do that before."

She pried his paws from around her neck and held him back up to eye level, and he leaned in and licked her face all over.

"So, should I put your name on him?" Rick asked.

"Hang on, let me try something," Kathleen replied.

The puppy had latched onto her neck again, and she pried him off and set him back in the kennel where he began to throw himself at the gate, whimpering and barking.

"Now? Shall I put your name on him now?"

 Kathleen cracked open the door again, and while all the other puppies ignored her, the little brown one squeezed through the opening, raced back onto her lap, climbed right up her jacket and grabbed her around the neck again, sobbing the entire time.

"Now?" Rick asked.

"OK," Kathleen replied. "Now."

Puppies are never allowed to leave the pound until they are eight-weeks old, so Kathleen kissed her new dog goodbye and told Rick she would visit him every week until she could finally bring him home to the farm. Her heart broke when she left him whimpering at the gate, but she promised she would return soon.

Ragano never forgot the moment when Kathleen finally found him. His earliest memory was of knowing there was a human he was supposed to take care of, and some nights, he would wander away from the rest of the litter and stare at the moon through the high kennel window and try to remember . . . because he knew he was supposed to remember what her face looked like . . . but it was so hard to picture. Yet the day Kathleen walked into the shelter and he'd glanced up from his place at the top of the puppy pile, he instantly recognized the very tall woman with the long, curly blonde hair; he felt as if he'd known her forever and ever. He couldn't understand why she didn't pick him up first, and he stared at her, willing her to notice him with all of his tiny puppy soul. When she finally lifted him out of the kennel he couldn't help himself, he had to hang onto her as tightly as he could and never let go!

The four long weeks slowly rolled past, and Kathleen visited as promised, until one day, she lifted him out of the puppy pile for the very last time and he finally rode home with her in the big, blue pickup truck.

At that time, old Rufus, a German shepherd mix who'd been taking care of Kathleen for almost seventeen years, was still alive, and he spent the next five months teaching Ragano everything he needed to know about taking care of his mistress. Rufus taught him how to keep a close eye on the yard for intruders, how to stay right next to the heel of Kathleen's foot when she walked out on the farm, and to never, ever let her out of his sight. There were many other things Ragano taught himself, like how to open all the doors in the house, and if Kathleen thought she could ever be on the opposite side of a door from her puppy, she quickly learned it was not the case. He also learned how to jump high fences and leap onto the old farm table in the kitchen, so if Kathleen ventured out into the yard without him he could watch her every move through the kitchen window.

That night, in the quiet kitchen lit only by the heat lamp on the farm table, Ragano jumped straight up and landed on all four feet next to the guinea pig cage. The tiny piglet slowly lifted his head and blinked his eyes several times. Then he stood up and walked to the bars of his cage and lifted his pink nose. Ragano leaned down and touched his nose to the pig's and gave a few sniffs.

"Hello," Ragano said.

"Hello," the piglet said.

"What are you?" the dog asked.

The piglet grinned, puffed out his tiny chest and proudly announced, "I'm a rock star!"

"I'm Ragano," the dog replied. "I'm a farm dog."

"What did he say?" Agnes asked from her spot on the floor. She jumped up and down, which she was very good at, but she couldn't get any forward momentum. She was also a very small dog, and only three months old.

"I'll be right back," Ragano said, and jumped to the tile floor.

He was a very clever boy, and as quietly as he could he pushed a kitchen chair away from the table. Then he pushed one of the tall stools away from the counter and lined them up next to each other.

"Here you go, Aggie," Ragano said. "Climb on the low one and then to the taller one and you'll be right up there with us."

Agnes struggled to get onto the chair, but Ragano gave her a boost with his muzzle, and in no time at all she, too, was nose-to-nose with the rock star pig.

"Hello," she said. "I'm Agnes."

"And I'm a rock star!" the little pig said. "But they call me Ozzie."

The two of them stared at each other. Agnes wasn't much bigger than he was, and when Ozzie smiled at her, she smiled right back, showing jagged teeth that came from having a cleft palate and hair lip, a condition she was born with.

"I like your smile," Ozzie said. "It's different, and it's happy!"

"Kathleen says it makes me extra special," Agnes said.

"Who's Kathleen?" Ozzie asked.

"The one who takes care of us," Agnes replied.

"Oh!" Ozzie said. "You mean Mama!"

"Well, I guess so," Agnes replied.

"Where are you from?" Ragano asked.

He had joined them back on the table.

"Someplace else," Ozzie replied. "But I'm here now!"

The piglet was so happy and excited he began to dance in his cage, but moments later his back legs went out from beneath him, each one sliding in its own direction.

"Oops!" he giggled, and struggled to get back up. "That keeps happening."

After a few tries, Ozzie got his back feet beneath him where they belonged and stood nose-to-nose with Agnes again.

"Mama says I have something called . . . um . . . splay leg . . . that makes me fall down like that," Ozzie said. "But I just get back up again."

And he cheerfully shook a few pine shavings off his back.

"And I have a crooked smile!" Agnes said. "Look at that! We're both extra special!"

The door to the kitchen creaked open, and Kathleen walked in to find her two dogs standing on the table with their noses pressed against Ozzie's cage.

"What in the world?" she gasped. "I was wondering where you two had disappeared to!"

"Mama! Mama!" Ozzie cried out and put his tiny feet on the bars of the cage. "Mama!"

Kathleen scooped Agnes off the table and set her on the floor,  and Ragano jumped down alongside her.

"What are you squealing about, Osboar? Are you OK?" she asked. She opened the top of the cage and lifted him out, then gave him a gentle kiss on the nose. "You go back to sleep, little boy. Don't you let these silly dogs bother you. You need lots of rest so you can get healthy."

She set him back in the cage and closed it, then picked Agnes up and tucked her under her arm. "Do I have to lock the bedroom door now?" she asked, and carried the puppy back up the bedroom stairs with Ragano at her heels.

Later, when they were snuggled together at the end of the big bed with David and Kathleen asleep near them, Agnes whispered into Ragano's ear, "I like Ozzie, Ragano," she said. "Do you think he'll be my friend?"

"Of course he will," Ragano replied. "Who wouldn't want to be your friend?"

Ozzie Osboar peeked over the side of his cage. The room was quiet, and no one else was awake. There were cats curled up on the rug in front of the kitchen sink, but they ignored him the way they seemed to ignore everyone unless they were hungry. He stretched out beneath the warmth of the heat lamp. The shavings were soft and smelled clean and fresh, his tummy was still full from the bottle he'd had before bed. He closed his eyes and pictured his mama's face smiling over him. His tummy, which had felt quite sick earlier in the day, was feeling much better. He was just a tiny little boy in a small cage on a table, but he already knew he was exactly where he wanted to stay forever.

Ozzie meeting the sheep

Chapter Two

What's a pig?

Few of the animals on Locket's Meadow had ever seen a pig before. They all knew one had arrived on the farm, but the word "pig" meant nothing to them. Calypso, the old lesson pony, had lived on many farms before she finally found her way home, and she'd only ever seen one pig at a distance, but she remembered it as being a huge, heavy animal.

"If a pig is what I'd seen, how could it be living in the kitchen of that little house?" Calypso wondered aloud to the other animals in her paddock.

She stomped her white-stockinged foot and sent a pair of flies buzzing away, but they quickly returned and she stomped again, then swished her black tail to send a few more on their way.

"I have heard of 'eating like a pig,'" said Classy, the lovely, old grey Arabian mare. "I don't think it's a compliment. I can't imagine Kathleen would want a sloppy eater in the house."

Cressida, the cranky little white and brown paint pony, snorted. "What haven't they had in that kitchen? Chickens, roosters, that big goose, goats. What's difference would one more animal make in that little house?"

Doc, the old mama goat, lifted her head from the scraps of hay she was sifting through in the stall she shared with her daughter, Ezzie.

"They kept pigs at the farm where I lived before I came here," Doc said. "They got one in the spring, and it disappeared in the fall. Every year."

"Where did they go to, Mama?" asked Ezzie.

"I don't know," Doc replied. "No one would ever say. The goats were kept in a different part of the farm, but I do remember them being rather sizable animals."

"I suppose we just have to wait for someone to come outside and tell us," Locket said. "Ragano will be here soon to do chores with Kathleen. He'll know."

Locket smiled as she said Ragano's name. She loved the young dog more than she could ever say, and she looked forward to his arrival each morning.

The sun had just popped over the horizon, lighting the tops of the trees that lined the back of the paddock and turning them a pale shade of gold. Percival the goose honked from the little side yard of the house and was answered by the ducks. Other than that, all was peaceful, until . . .

"Carlos! Carlyle! Carlita! You get back here right now!"

Everyone in the barnyard swung their heads in the direction of the yelling. Calypso sighed.

"Carl got what he had coming to him," she said.

Three young crows swooped past them and raced to the huge pine tree behind the farmhouse, followed by another lone crow yelling at the top of his lungs.

"Do you hear me?" the crow screamed again.

The three young ones skirted the pine tree and flew back towards the barn, diving down and entering through the double doors to cut through the aisle, but before they could escape out the other side, a fifth crow dove in from the opposite doorway and screeched at the top of her lungs.

"Stop. Right. There!!!" she yelled.

The three crows landed in a tangled heap of wings and feet. A few loose black feathers drifted to the floor.

"Oh, hello Grandmother Carla!" said Carlita. She collected herself and offered a small curtsy. "Good morning!"

"Don't you 'good morning' me, young lady," Carla scolded. "You were in the indoor riding arena breaking up a sparrow's nest with your brothers. What have I told you about leaving other bird's nests alone?"

"But Grandmother, all the babies have flown away and they're done with it . . ."

"Don't you argue with me," Carla said. "It's disrespectful. And you!" Carla glared at the two boys who had scrambled to attention. "Your mother is waiting for you back at the nest. Get going!"

"Yes, Grandmother Carla," they replied, and the three of them quickly flapped out of the barn and headed for their home in a tall tree on the other side of the farm behind the horse barn.

Carla glanced over at her son, who, when he'd seen his mother dive through the open doorway, had landed on a stall door and waited. He knew his mother would handle his wayward children much more quickly and thoroughly than he ever could.

"Thank you, Mother," Carl said. "They're a handful."

"It's a mother's revenge," Carla replied. "Whatever behavior you tortured your mother with comes right back to you when you have children of your own."

"Times three," Carl sighed.

"Well, yes," Carla smiled. "If that's what you deserve."

"I have to get back to the nest and back up Bettina while she grounds them," Carl said. "They won't be leaving the tree any time soon. Thanks again."

Carl took off after his children, and Carla hopped out of the barn and onto a fence post.

Cressida snickered while the others politely hid their smiles. Carla, however, chuckled out loud.

"Oh, that boy," Carla said. "What he put me through when he was young! It's a miracle I don't have grey feathers."

"This is true," old Calypso said. "It's been a few years coming, but he's finally getting what he paid for." She paused, then added, "Not that you didn't do an excellent job of raising him. Some kids are just born with . . . spunk."

"You are kind," Carla said. "If it had only just been 'spunk.' So," she added, ruffling her feathers and settling them again into a smooth, shiny coat, "I must change the subject. What is this I hear about a pig in the farmhouse kitchen?"

"That's what we heard," Locket said. "Not that any of us have really seen a pig before. We're waiting for news from Ragano."

"Huh!" Carla said. "I've seen a few, but never had a conversation with one. I suppose we will all learn a thing or two about them soon enough. They do grow to be large animals, though."

"Wait!" Classy said. "Listen!"

The back door had opened and slammed shut, and they turned to watch Ragano run to the top of the tallest rock in the flowerbed, leap over the fence and race to the barn. Agnes, who was much too small to jump that high, stayed behind the white picket fence.

Locket smiled. She remembered a duck who once lived on Locket's Meadow who had also taken many mighty leaps from the top of that rock, flapping as hard as he could to get over the fence and then waddling to the barn to visit with her. Ragano, however, leaped with the grace of a deer, clearing the top with plenty of room to spare.

"Locket!" Ragano yelled as he raced into the barn at lightning speed. "Locket! Guess what!"

"There's a pig in the kitchen?" Locket responded.

"There is! There is!" Ragano said. "He's pink and tiny and he's in a little cage on top of the kitchen table. Agnes and I snuck downstairs to visit him last night."

"What's he like?" asked Calypso. "Is he nice?"

"He was very nice to us," Ragano said. "He said he's a rock star, but we could call him Ozzie. Mama says his whole name is Ozzie Osboar."

"Mama?" Classy said.

"I mean Kathleen," Ragano said. "But Ozzie calls her Mama. She's feeding him a bottle right now. Oh, and he says he has something called . . . I don't remember, but it makes his legs slide and he falls down. But he gets right back up again and laughs. I really, really like him!"

"He sounds like a perfect addition to the farm," Locket smiled again.

"Oh, but Mama . . . Kathleen, I mean . . . said he's sick and we have to be careful with him," Ragano said.

"Sick?" Classy asked. "With what?"

"I don't know," Ragano said. "But here they come!"

He turned and raced back to the yard and lightly jumped back over the fence as Kathleen walked through the kitchen door carrying a tiny pink animal in one hand.

"That's a pig?" Cressida snorted. "Seriously? That tiny thing is what all the fuss is about? It's no bigger than a kitten!"

But she watched as closely as the rest as Kathleen approached the barn carefully holding her new baby.

If you visit a farm and then go back a year later, things are seldom exactly the same. Animals come and go, people come and go, buildings change and fences get rearranged. Since they first bought the farm, a lot had happened at Locket's Meadow.

When Kathleen and David first started rescuing horses from slaughter they had no intention of finding homes for them; they planned to keep them right on their farm for the rest of their lives. But once they realized how many horses were in danger, they decided they needed to do much more. Two years after they first began to rescue, the couple decided to save many, many more horses, most of whom were adopted out to new homes. Sometimes one or two would stay, but most of them only lived on Locket's Meadow for a little while until their forever home could be found. More than a hundred horses had found their way through Locket's Meadow over the past few years, but the first group of rescues always stayed on, as they were now members of the family.

Other things had changed, as well. The barn girls, who came after school and exercised horses, grew older and moved on to new adventures, while younger children replaced them. Animals that had lived long and happy lives had grown old and died, and new rescues had arrived and settled in. Some of the horses that had once lived in the barn behind the little house had moved next door to the big barn so they wouldn't have to be fetched every time someone wanted to ride them or take a lesson.

With so many rescues coming through the farm, stalls that were usually reserved for boarding horses were needed for temporary residents, and so, a little at a time, the boarder horses left and were not replaced. Boarders were a source of income for the farm, so with fewer horses bringing in money, Kathleen and David needed to earn more money. Kathleen, who worked as a newspaper reporter, had taken a better paying job at a larger newspaper, which meant she had to work more hours. She could still write most of her stories from her office in the little farmhouse, but there were many more stories to write than before. Because she couldn't spend as much time in the barns as she used to, she'd hired a new barn manager, Bonnie, to keep an eye on the animals and make sure everyone was taken care of and safe.

Even with extra help, there was still much work to do, and early every morning as the sun rose Kathleen and David walked out to the barns to feed and water their animal friends and lead them out to their paddocks. On Ozzie Osboar's first day at Locket's Meadow, Kathleen decided to bring him outside with her so he could see the farm that was now his home.

"Come on, my little man," Kathleen said, wiping milk from her piglet's chin. "Time to meet the rest of the family. Some day you'll spend most of your time outside with them. I think you'll like everybody."

She wrapped him in a tiny, pink, fleece blanket and Ozzie gave a happy squeal.

Kathleen arrived at the barn, Ragano circling at her feet, to find all the animals leaning over the tops of their stalls, eyes fixed on her. A large crow that was perched on the top of Classy's stall door gave a loud caw and quickly flapped away.

"Good morning, my angels!" Kathleen said. "Look what we have!"

She held Ozzie up for everyone to see and he smiled and giggled.

"We've never had a pig before, but I guess it's about time!" she said, and brought him down level with her face so she could kiss him on the nose.

Classy nickered. She had spotted Bonnie, the barn manager, walking up the path towards them. Bonnie was a tall, broad woman with dark hair and a very red face.

"Good morning!" Bonnie said as she entered the small barn. "Is that our new little resident?"

"Yes, it's Ozzie Osboar," Kathleen replied. "Isn't he perfect?"

"He's so tiny," Bonnie said. "You'll have to keep a close eye on him. People around here like to have pig roasts."

"What?" Kathleen stepped back in horror. "Are you suggesting someone would steal my pig for food? He's a pet!"

"You never know," Bonnie said. "People can be mean."

"Well," Kathleen replied, "not on this farm, they can't. Don't even talk like that in front of my babies."

"I'm sorry," Bonnie said. "I just stopped over to tell you I already brought Falstaff next door and fed him. I'm taking him for an early ride today to the airport grounds."

There was a huge, grassy field about a half mile away that at one time had been a small airport but now had soccer fields and outdoor riding arenas filled with deep sand. The townspeople called it the airport, but no planes had landed there for many decades.

"Sure, that's fine," Kathleen said. "I'll be working from home today. I have a ton of articles to write, and I need to keep a close eye on Ozzie. I'm adjusting the concentration of his milk replacer to see if I can get his diarrhea under control."

19

"Sounds like a fun day," Bonnie said. "I'll be back in a few hours."

She stopped and gently pet Locket on her way back to the big barn.

Kathleen shook her head. "Why would she say something like that?" she wondered aloud. "Everyone knows we don't eat any animals here – we rescue them from being eaten! So odd."

She held her little piglet just a little tighter.

"Ah, well. Calypso! Locket!" Kathleen said, smiling, "Have you ever met a piglet before? Here he is, our very own rock star, Ozzie Osboar!"

And one at a time, she presented the grinning little piglet to everyone in the barn.

Bonnie walked back to the big barn and took Falstaff from a stall and tied him in the aisle. He was a very large, very handsome, draft-cross, bay paint with white and black markings. She began to groom him, gripping the hard, wooden brush in her right hand as she knocked the dirt from his legs. Falstaff stamped one of his large feet to get rid of a biting fly.

"Knock it off," Bonnie said.

Falstaff stood quietly while she worked on cleaning his front leg, but a horse fly had landed on his stomach and pierced his skin, so he lifted a rear leg and tapped his foot against his belly to get rid of it.

"I said, knock it off!" Bonnie growled at him, then took the wooden brush, drew her arm all the way back and slammed the edge of the brush against his cheek with all her might.

Chapter Three

Swimming Sows

K athleen stood at the kitchen island eating a tomato and reading her email before sitting down to write her articles for the day. Ozzie was inches away, asleep in his guinea pig cage. She clicked on an email from Farm Sanctuary, a large animal rescue and sanctuary in New York State, and gasped.

"What's the matter?" David asked from the kitchen table where he was finishing his breakfast and writing his work list for the day.

"Why didn't I know about this?" Kathleen said as she scanned the email. "There was a huge flood in Iowa in June, and thousands of pigs drowned! You know, the ones that are kept in those horrible cages. They drowned. Thousands of them! Farm Sanctuary rescued sixty-nine of them, brought them back to New York, and now they're looking for adoptive homes."

"Oh no," David said. "I see we've opened up a fine kettle of fish here. Can't we have just one little pig for now?"

"David, the ones that managed to escape swam to a levee and stood on it in the hot sun," Kathleen said, tears welling in her eyes. "Some of the mama pigs gave birth right there and were desperately trying to protect their babies, standing over them so they wouldn't get sunburned. And then the people in the area were worried they'd break the levee so they went out on boats with rifles and started shooting them! Why didn't I read this in the news?"

Kathleen clicked out of her email and typed "pigs flooding Iowa" into a search engine and quickly found a list of articles. The first one was an interview with a farmer who said even the pigs that had survived had to be destroyed because their meat was contaminated by the polluted floodwaters. She read some of it out loud to David, then said, "Can you imagine escaping from one of those horrible gestation crates, swimming a mile to a levee, surviving being shot at only to have someone kill you because they can't eat you anymore? Even the survivors were killed! How is that fair?"

Kathleen opened Ozzie's cage, lifted out the tiny pig and tucked him under her chin. The piglet opened his eyes for a moment and smiled, then snuggled up into the crook of his mama's neck and dozed off again.

David set his cup of coffee down on the table and looked up from his list. He already knew there was nothing he could do to stop his wife from getting involved; there she was, with that pink piglet tucked up against her neck, eyes glistening with tears, and he knew there was only one thing to say.

"Give Farm Sanctuary a call, and see what we have to do," he said. "I have to get to the office."

He stood and reached for his car keys, but they weren't on the hook where he'd left them the night before.

"Good grief!" he mumbled. "Where did he put them this time?"

Kathleen looked up from her research.

"Check inside the fridge," she said. "That's where I found the truck keys yesterday."

David opened the refrigerator door and stared inside.

"Produce drawer," Kathleen said.

"Got 'em," David replied, reaching in and picking his keys out from between the celery and onions. "He's a creative ghost, I'll give him that."

Kathleen nodded. Over the years they had become quite familiar with their farm ghost, who loved to play pranks on the residents. They had long ago realized he was a harmless spirit trying to have fun, but there were often times when his sense of humor was frustrating, especially when they were in a hurry. His fondness for opening stall doors and letting animals out had also caused a lot of commotion for the couple.

"Call me and let me know what you find out from Farm Sanctuary," David said, leaning down to kiss Kathleen goodbye. "I'll be in my office all day."

He walked to the door and Kathleen quickly returned to her online research about the terrors of being a pig caught in a massive flood.

There had been a huge ruckus in the crows' tree when the young ones returned from their most recent round of troublemaking, and their mother was furious. The arguing went on for hours.

"This is your fault!" Bettina shouted at Carl. "If you didn't fill their heads with stories of the exploits of Carl and Wilson in your youth they wouldn't think of doing these things!"

"Now, Bettina," Carl said, "I'm pretty sure they'd think of ways to get into trouble without any suggestions from me or their Uncle Wilson."

"How am I supposed to protect them until they're grown if you keep encouraging them to do ridiculous things?" Bettina shouted.

"I . . . um . . . was that a raindrop I just felt?" Carl mumbled, looking at the sky.

Later, when Carl and Bettina left the family tree to fetch some lunch, Carlos and Carlyle battled furiously over who got to perch on the highest branch. Carlita, as she often did, grew antsy. Like her brothers, she was grounded and forbidden to fly, but, well, the boys were being boring. She decided she'd help her mother out by finding her own lunch, so she checked to make sure neither parent was in sight and swooped down to the ground near the big barn double doors to scratch around in the dirt for bugs. She picked a fat, white grub out of the ground and gobbled it down, and was reaching for a worm when she heard a woman's voice and looked up to see Bonnie, the barn manager, smack Falstaff on the face. Carla froze in horror. Everyone knew no one was allowed to hit anyone on Locket's Meadow. It was Kathleen's number-one rule.

Bonnie raised the brush up to Falstaff's eyes and said, "Behave yourself or I'll smack you again!" Then she turned and walked into the tack room.

Carlita quickly flew into the barn and landed in front of the big horse.

"Falstaff, are you OK?" she asked.

"I'm fine," he replied, but the look in his eyes told the young crow he was not fine at all.

"Why didn't you bite her?" Carlita asked. "That's what I would have done! How dare she hit you!?"

"It's not the first time," Falstaff said. "Don't worry. I know how to deal with her. Now go, little girl. She's just getting her saddle, so she'll be right back."

He reached his nose down as far as the cross ties let him and gently nudged her. "Hurry up! I can handle this."

Carlita heard the tack room doorknob turn and she scooted between Falstaff's legs before taking flight and swooshing out the big doors at the opposite end of the barn. She shot straight up over the barn roof and landed back in the family tree where Carlos and Carlyle were still arguing over the uppermost branch.

"I'm the biggest, baddest crow on Locket's Meadow!" Carlos shouted and slammed into his brother, who held on tightly, but lost his balance and flipped upside down.

"Hey!" Carlyle shouted, but didn't let go and flapped his wings until he was upright again. "Can't knock me down! I'm badder!"

Carlita flapped onto the branch and landed between them.

"Move it, sister!" Carlos said. "It's time for this bad boy to be top bird!"

"Never mind your stupid game," Carlita said. "I just saw something really bad! Wait 'til you hear this!"

Few people thought of Falstaff as a particularly clever horse, but they were wrong. Only the cleverest horse would carefully hide how very smart he really was. Falstaff stood calmly in the aisle while Bonnie set her saddle on his back and tightened the girth. He was completely composed when she lifted the bridle over his head and slipped the bit into his mouth. He didn't move a muscle as she tightened the chinstrap.

"I see you've learned your lesson," Bonnie said, smiling smugly. "Don't ever upset me again. I'm the boss here."

Falstaff stood perfectly still at the mounting block and didn't flinch when a horsefly attached to his belly and bit deeply through his hide. Bonnie slid onto the saddle, and they rode to the end of the driveway and turned onto Old Litchfield Turnpike to head towards the airport. Falstaff's face stung where she'd hit him, but that didn't distract him from thinking about the plan he had for Bonnie.

Kathleen took a break from writing and stood in the yard watching Agnes and Ozzie chase each other around the Japanese maple tree.

She smiled at how quickly the two had become best friends. Ragano sat next to Kathleen and watched as well. He also smiled as the two tiny buddies tumbled over each other, bumped heads and then sped off up the hill, laughing the entire time.

"Who would have thought it?" Kathleen said to Ragano, stroking the top of his head. "A pig and a puppy become best friends, just like that!" and she snapped her fingers.

Agnes chased Ozzie into the tall wildflower garden at the top of the hill, and a pair of hummingbirds darted away from the red bee balm where they were hovering. Moments later Agnes burst from a clump of daisies with Ozzie in close pursuit. They raced back down the hill to the maple tree and flopped on the ground, caught their breath for a minute, then took off again at top speed.

Kathleen and Ragano turned their heads toward the sound of horseshoes clip-clopping on pavement. Kathleen waved at Bonnie and Falstaff as they walked past the house on their way to the airport, then Kathleen turned and called to Ozzie.

"Come on, Osboar!" she said. "Mama's got to get this article done and sent to the office. I have to give you another bottle so I can get back to work!"

Ozzie raced to her, squealing his happy squeal the entire way.

Kathleen picked him up and rubbed her forehead against his round belly, chanting, "Piggy, piggy, piggy, piggy! All that running must have made you hungry. I have warm milk waiting for you in the kitchen."

Falstaff was a very good boy when Bonnie asked him to trot the first lap around the airport. He was a good boy when she asked him to canter the second lap. The third lap, when she asked him to gallop, he was also a very good boy . . . at least until he reached the farthest corner, as far away from the farm as a horse could go before he would have to step into the woods. And that was the precise moment he pulled together every muscle in his big, strong body and threw the biggest buck he'd ever managed in his entire life . . . the biggest . . . buck . . . ever.

Classy had finished up the last of the morning's hay and was standing next to Calypso, noses to tails, so they could swish the persistent August flies away from each other's faces. Locket stood nearby where she could see the back door of the little house, just in case it opened and Ragano was let outside to play. Cranky Cressida and the goats were curled up in the shed taking their morning naps. All was quiet . . . for a few moments . . .

Classy lifted her head. She heard horseshoes pounding on pavement, galloping up the street towards the house.

"What in the world is that?" she muttered. A horse running on pavement was never a good thing. Moments later she gasped.

"Look!" she called to the rest of the paddock.

The others lifted their heads and saw Falstaff racing towards the house at a dead run. His saddle was empty and the loose stirrups slapped against his belly with each huge stride. When he reached the driveway he took a left turn into the yard, slowed to a trot, and made a beeline right to his stall where he stood, heaving to catch his breath, chest covered with foamy sweat.

"Well, nothing about that can possibly be good," Cressida mumbled.

Ragano

Chapter Four

Spies Like Us

Kathleen was writing a story about high bacteria counts in local swimming areas. Ozzie was wrapped in a fleece baby blanket sleeping soundly on her lap, while Agnes and Ragano sprawled on the floor at her feet. Kathleen wasn't thinking about bacteria; mostly she thought about the phone call she'd just had with a woman from Farm Sanctuary named Susie Coston, who'd told her they were actively searching for new homes for the rescued Iowa pigs.

"One thing we have to be sure of," Susie said, "is that there's no chance these pigs will be slaughtered for food."

"Oh no!" Kathleen had replied, horrified. "We would never do that. We're all vegetarians here, and we've been rescuing animals from slaughterhouses for years. Mostly horses, of course, but we recently got our first pig and I just realized I absolutely love them!"

Susie had laughed and said she understood; she loved them, too. Kathleen told her she could research information about Locket's Meadow on the internet, and hopefully then she'd understand. So now, she sat with her piglet snuggled in her lap and waited. She thought about how much the pigs from Iowa had suffered, and how they deserved to have a safe and happy life, and she knew she could give that to one of them on Locket's Meadow.

Her phone rang and she quickly answered.

"Hello?"

"Hey darlin'," said David.

"Oh, it's you," Kathleen replied. "I was hoping it was Farm Sanctuary."

"No word yet?" he asked.

"Nope," she replied. "I'm trying to work, but I can't concentrate. Wouldn't it be nice for Osboar to have another pig here to keep him company?"

"I'm not sure Ozzie needs any more than you and the dogs," David said. "You seem to do just fine. But I'm sure they'll let us adopt one. I can't imagine many people are standing in line for pet pigs."

"Maybe not," Kathleen replied. "I'll call you when I know something."

She hung up and turned back to her notebook to try and focus on acceptable bacteria levels, but it wasn't easy.

"Falstaff!" Classy called over the top half of his stall that was open to the paddock. "Falstaff! What happened? Where's Bonnie?"

But Falstaff stood silent, stoically waiting.

For what? Classy thought. She'd never seen anything like this before.

Classy Pony

She and the other ladies of the paddock stood nearby, silent and worried. Drops of sweat fell from Falstaff's chest as his breathing slowly returned to normal, and Classy knew he must be desperate to have his tack removed and have a nice cool shower in the wash stall.

Locket whispered, "Something terrible must have happened. Falstaff would never run away if his rider fell off. He'd never leave their side."

"I know," Classy whispered back.

Calypso, the old lesson pony, said nothing. She was a smart, old lady who'd lived on a lot of farms and she'd had a bad feeling that Bonnie wasn't as nice as she pretended to be. She'd kept quiet, hoping she was wrong. Today, she thought, would reveal the truth, either way.

Bonnie finally trudged up the driveway and into the barn. The ponies and Locket saw her coming, pants covered with dirt and grass stains, and they stepped back from Falstaff's door.

"Oh, you are a lucky boy, Sir John Falstaff," she spat at the sweaty horse. "So lucky."

She stepped into his stall and roughly removed his tack. Falstaff stiffened his legs and didn't move a muscle no matter how hard she tried to shove him around as she unfastened his girth. She slapped his belly with the loosened end, stinging him with the buckle. "So lucky you're over here where your mama can protect you. But wait. Just wait. I'll get you next door tomorrow, and we'll settle this, you and I. Nobody does this to me. Nobody!"

She unfastened his bridle and yanked the bit from his mouth, banging it against his teeth. "Another time, my friend. Another time. We will settle this . . .," Bonnie growled between her teeth.

Falstaff stood stock still, not batting an eye or moving a muscle.

"Think you're tough, big boy?" Bonnie said. "I guess we'll find out who's tougher."

She piled the bridle and saddle pad, drenched with sweat, on top of the saddle and slammed the stall door closed.

"Tomorrow," she said, and glared long and hard at him before she turned and walked away.

Falstaff was soaked with salty sweat, and it stung as it dripped into his eyes, but he didn't care. All he could think about was his rage, and how he would never, ever let that woman break his spirit.

"Falstaff," Classy whispered. "Are you OK?"

The big paint horse finally relaxed his stance and began to tremble.

"No. No I'm not," he replied. "But believe me, I will be."

And thus began the epic battle of Locket's Meadow: Bonnie versus Falstaff. To the finish.

Carlos and Carlyle listened with horror to Carlita's story about how Bonnie had treated Falstaff.

"If I was there, I would have dived down and pecked at her eyes!" Carlyle said.

"If I was there, I . . . I . . . I would have done something, too!" Carlos said. "We have to tell Mom and Dad when they get back!"

"No!" Carlita said. "Then they'll know I left the tree! I'm already in enough trouble."

"But she can't do that to Falstaff," Carlyle said. "Nobody can do that to anyone!"

"Should we tell Grandmother?" Carlos asked.

"NO!" both Carlita and Carlyle said.

Everyone was a little frightened of Carla, with good reason. A scolding from her stuck with you for months, maybe even forever. Their father had told them stories of how Bingo and Star had arrived on the farm as unruly colts, but twenty minutes of "what-for" from Carla straightened them out after months of training by humans had done nothing.

"So a bad person can get away with being bad?" Carlos said.

"No," Carlita said. "Look, we're eventually going to get off punishment. What if we do some investigating? You know, collect evidence, and then . . . then we figure out what to do with it."

"Like spies?" Carlyle asked

"Yes! Like spies!" Carlita replied.

"And then what?" Carlos asked.

31

"I don't know yet," Carlita replied. "I guess we'll figure that out when we get to it."

Kathleen had just finished writing her last story of the day, but she still hadn't heard back from Farm Sanctuary.

"Ah well, Osboar," she said, holding him up to her face and kissing him on his tiny pink nose. "Maybe tomorrow."

Ozzie smiled and squealed. He loved it when his Mama held him up high in the air and gave him kisses and belly nuzzles.

"Time to hang out in your cage for a little while," Kathleen said. "Mama has to get a little fresh air and check on the barn."

Kathleen gently placed Ozzie in the guinea pig cage and put her work boots on. Ragano knew that was the signal for a visit to the barn, and he ran to the door and waited for Kathleen to finish tying her shoelaces. She opened the back door and in three bounds the dog had flown out the door and over the fence, reaching the barn doors in seconds and racing out the other side to the paddock.

"Locket!" Ragano shouted. "Locket! Mama . . . Kathleen . . . oh, Mama . . . Mama says we may be getting a new pig! A full-grown big pig that needs to be rescued!"

Locket walked up to the fence and touched noses with her friend.

"Well, wouldn't that be exciting?" she said.

But Ragano knew his friend well, and could tell there was something wrong.

"What's the matter, Locket?" he asked.

"Nothing," Locket said. "Nothing for you to worry about, at least."

But something *was* the matter. Ragano heard Kathleen in the barn and she sounded mad.

"Why are you in your stall and who left you like this?" Kathleen said. "Look at you!"

Locket glanced at the barn doors, and Ragano turned and ran back inside.

"Falstaff, why didn't you get hosed off after your ride?" Kathleen said. "You still have saddle pad and girth marks on you!"

She went into his stall and traced the little rivers of dried salt that ran down his belly with her finger.

"Hang on, angel," she said. "I'll hose you down in a minute."

She took her cell phone from the back pocket of her jeans and dialed.

"Bonnie?" she said when the barn manager picked up the phone.

"Hi, Kathleen," Bonnie replied. "What's up?"

"Why didn't you hose Falstaff down after your ride? He's a mess!"

"Of course I hosed him down," Bonnie replied. "He was so sweaty, we worked hard up at the airport."

"Bonnie, that's impossible. He has saddle pad marks on him and he's sticky with salt and sweat!"

"I absolutely cleaned him up," Bonnie replied. "Of course, he may have continued to sweat after I put him in his stall. That would explain it."

"But you can't put a horse away hot! He should have been walked out and then turned out in his paddock."

"He seemed cool enough to me," Bonnie replied. "And I've been doing this long enough to know. Maybe something upset him in his stall."

"That's impossible. I'd have heard," Kathleen replied. "I've been working in the house all day, and I can hear from my office. And look! He has a big lump on his cheekbone. It's all swollen!"

"I really don't know what happened," Bonnie said. "You know, this wouldn't happen if he didn't live on your side of the farm. If he had a stall and a paddock over here, I could keep a better eye on him. You know, in case something upset him in his stall and he banged his face and started to sweat . . ."

"Falstaff? Leave my back yard? He can't possibly be separated from James and Captain."

"They should all be over here," Bonnie said. "It would be so much easier to exercise and train them."

"I don't know," Kathleen said. "I'd have to think about it."

"It's up to you," Bonnie replied. "I've been working with horses my entire life, so I do know what I'm doing. Of course, I've never been fortunate enough to own one of my own. You are a lucky woman to have so many."

"I suppose I am, but that's not what . . ."

"I have a rider waiting for a lesson in the arena, so I have to go," Bonnie said. "I'll catch up with you later."

Bonnie hung up the phone and Kathleen reached for Falstaff's halter to take him out in the yard and let him graze while she hosed him off. She was upset and confused, yet Bonnie had been so adamant she'd done her job.

"I don't know, Fally," she said. "It just seems impossible to me."

Ragano raced back to Locket.

"You know what happened, don't you?" Ragano asked.

"Yes," Locket replied. "And it's very, very bad."

Locket quickly told Ragano the story.

"What do we do?" Ragano asked.

"I don't know," Locket said. "Falstaff seems to think he has this under control, but so does Bonnie."

Kathleen's cell phone rang, and Ragano ran back to where she was hosing down Falstaff on the grassy lawn. She turned off the water and answered.

"Hello?"

"Hi Kathleen, it's Susie from Farm Sanctuary."

"Oh! Susie!" Kathleen replied. "So good to hear from you! What did you decide?"

"Well, we looked up your farm online and read some of the articles about the work you do, and we decided you are perfect candidates to adopt a pig from us."

"Oh wonderful!" Kathleen said. "I'm so excited!"

"There's just one thing," Susie said. "I know you asked about taking one pig, but we have this very special pair of bonded females. They were both desperately sick when we rescued them, and they've been at Cornell Veterinary Hospital for quite a while. They refused to be apart from each other, and with all they'd been through, well, we do want to make sure they stay together."

"Two?" Kathleen said. "Two pigs. My goodness. We just got our very first, and we'd jump right up to three."

"Is that too much?" Susie asked.

Kathleen knew she should say that she needed to check with her husband first, but . . .

"You know," she said, "the more the merrier. I think two more pigs would be just fine."

"OK," Susie said. "Can we deliver them in two weeks? Depending on their health, of course."

"Absolutely," Kathleen replied.

She hung up the phone and reached for the hose.

"I may be in trouble, Falstaff," she said, aiming the stream of water at the salt trails on his hip.

Ragano raced back through the barn and out to Locket.

"Two! Two!"

"What are you yelling about?" asked Cressida, who had joined Locket at the fence.

"Mama says we're getting two more pigs on Locket's Meadow!" Ragano shouted, leaping into the air. "Two is so much better than one! I love pigs!!!"

"Well, now you know it, I know it and the entire neighborhood knows it," Cressida said. "Shout a little louder, and the whole world will know."

"I think I will!" Ragano jumped again with joy. "TWO PIGS! Yay!"

And Locket, who was still worried about Falstaff, couldn't help but smile in spite of her fears.

Locket, front, Cressida, behind

Chapter Five

Hearing Voices

L ocket smiled and congratulated Ragano, but if she wore sleeves, she'd have had a secret . . . or two . . . tucked away in them. She'd already known there were two pigs trying to find their way to Locket's Meadow, and she'd been "chatting" with them for several weeks. Locket, you see, had some very special gifts. She could communicate with other animals who weren't even near the farm, and she could also see and hear ghosts. From the time she'd first arrived on the farm she was able to see the resident ghost, Michael, and over the years they became very good friends. But there was more to Locket's gifts than that . . .

One day, the little burro heard the voice of a frightened little filly from far, far away. The filly's name was Beatrice, and the little horse was in trouble in a distant land called Canada. She eventually found her way to Locket's Meadow along with rescued colts Bart and Benny. Soon after hearing Beatrice, Locket also heard the deep and patient voice of Ernie, the giant draft colt from North Dakota, who also became a permanent resident of the farm. And later, when the huge Muscovy duck named Duck, her dearest friend, died, she didn't have time to mourn him as he immediately showed up in her stall, the most exuberant ghost she'd ever seen, spinning around her head, chatting and laughing until she almost toppled over from dizziness. The last time she'd seen him he'd stopped by to tell her he was going to study with a spirit who would teach him how to come back and live another life. This time, he insisted he'd return as an animal who could live in the house. Months later, when Ragano arrived, Locket knew right away who he was and who he had been, but she'd also kept that secret tightly locked away. Duck had told her that when he returned he wouldn't be able to remember anything from his previous life on the farm, but their bond of love had been so strong they recognized each other right away. They never spoke of it, and Locket wasn't sure how much Ragano remembered, but she knew . . . and she remembered everything.

Having these abilities was an awesome responsibility for a little burro to carry, and sometimes, as much as she loved the other ladies in her paddock, it felt like more than she could share with them.

It was very early one morning, under the glow of a full moon, when she'd first heard the voices of the Sisters, as she came to call them. The rest of the horses were sleeping. On the evening of the full moon they always spent the night dancing in their paddocks to the music of the stars, and they had finished up and were very tired.

"Sister," a voice had said. "Sister, I do believe there is someone listening to us."

"We are the only ones in this stall, Sister," said the other voice, "and it's late at night. Who could possibly be eavesdropping?"

"Now, now Sister, I am convinced of it!" the first voice said. "Who are you? Who are you, and don't play games with us!"

"I am Locket," the burro replied. "I live on Locket's Meadow, and I apologize. I never mean to hear what I hear. Sometimes it just happens. You can speak with me if you like, or not if you prefer. But usually, if I hear you, it means we're supposed to know each other."

"You sound so far away! But I forget myself," she said. "I am being quite rude. Let me introduce ourselves. I am Harriet, and this is my sister, Ice."

"Pleased to meet you," Locket said. "What kind of animal are you?"

"Delighted to meet you," said Ice. "And we are sows. Lady pigs. And we are always ladies."

"May I ask a question?" Locket said.

"Of course," Harriet replied.

"Usually when I hear voices it means the animals talking to me are in need of rescuing," Locket said. "Do you need help?"

"Oh, no dear," said Ice. "You see, we have already been rescued. At least for now."

"Yes indeed," said Harriet. "From the raging waters. From the men with guns."

"From the metal cages and the burning sun," Ice said.

"From a life of pain, no more to run," Harriet added, and Locket smiled at the first of many rhymes the ladies would speak in. "At least we hope we won't be running anymore. Or swimming."

"Where are you?" Locket asked.

"Not a clue," said Harriet.

"No idea at all," said Ice. "But I believe it is a sort of infirmary, as we were quite ill when we were pulled from the waters. I was told I had pneumonia, and dear Sister had an infected foot. We have been here for weeks, and they have medicated us. We are much better now, but alas, no babies . . ."

"No babies . . ." said Harriet.

"No babies . . ." chanted the sisters together.

"They tried to separate us, but we put up a fight," Ice said. "We sisters swim together."

"Always together," Harriet added.

"So they let us share a stall, which is much nicer than what we lived in before," Ice said.

"Sometimes when I hear voices it's because they belong to animals who need to come here," Locket said.

"Where is here?" asked both ladies at once.

Locket told them about the farm that was named for her. She told them about the animals that came from all over the country, many from scary and dangerous places. She told them about Kathleen and David, who took care of them, and about the magic that seemed to watch over everyone.

"It sounds delightful!" Harriet said. "Sister, wouldn't it be nice to be at such a place, where there is grass and fresh water?"

"My, yes," Ice replied. "But are there any babies?"

"Sometimes we have baby horses," Locket said.

"No baby pigs?" Ice asked.

"No," Locket said. "I'm sorry. But it's still a very lovely place."

"How does one get to your meadow?" asked Harriet.

"The only way I've ever known is by wishing on the moon," Locket said. "Can you see it?"

"No window," the ladies said together.

"I am looking right at the most beautiful full moon," Locket said. "Would you like me to wish for you?"

"If you wouldn't mind," said Harriet.

"Yes, please," said Ice.

Locket stared at the moon and wished out loud for the sisters to find their way to Locket's Meadow, and the ladies politely thanked her and said they would like to retire for the night, leaving Locket to ponder many things, but especially, what on earth was a pig? She had kept that conversation, and several others with them that had followed, all to herself for the next few weeks, and on the morning when Ragano told her about the baby pig on the kitchen table she'd marveled at the magic of the farm.

The night before she'd wished again, all alone, on a waxing half moon, for the sisters to find their way home, and now, it seemed they were on their way, and she was almost as excited as Ragano. The others were asleep and she'd stood alone in the middle of the paddock, staring at the moon.

"Locket, my love!" said a voice from nowhere.

"Michael!" Locket said as the farm ghost materialized before her. "How have you been?"

"The same as always," Michael replied. "Aside from opening a few stalls now and then, hiding car keys, and maybe slamming a door and turning a few lights on in the middle of the night, it's been rather ho-hum."

"Halloween will come soon enough, and things will pick up," Locket said.

"This is true," he replied. "Alas, I'm afraid I have mellowed quite a bit. Remember the old days? You could get me all riled up then, couldn't you?"

"Yes," Locket said. "But we have done some good work together. Remember when you helped me escape from my stall so Duck and I could go next door and try to help poor, sad Beatrice?"

"Ah yes," Michael said. "And after that they put bungee cords on the stall doors for the longest time. Darn it, but I never could get the hang of unhooking a bungee. Elastic is tough, you know!"

Locket smiled. "So many adventures," she said. "We've been lucky to know each other."

"Locket!" Michael cried. "You make it sound as if we're all washed up! Silly burro. We have a few adventures left in us. Now, if you need me for anything, you know how to get me. Especially around Halloween. I'm at my very best then, you know."

"You know I will, old friend," Locket said. "I'm going to make one more wish on this moon, and then I'm going to get some sleep. You enjoy your evening!"

"I shall," Michael replied. "Goodnight, sweet burro!" he said and drifted out of sight.

Baby pigs grow very, very quickly, even runts, and Ozzie was no exception. By the end of the first week, Kathleen had mastered the correct concentration of milk replacer that was safe for his stomach, and he finally began to thrive. Meanwhile, he traveled with her everywhere on the farm in a little pink carrier designed for small dogs. In fact, it was the same one that Agnes had come home in several months earlier, tucked under an airplane seat, all the way from Indiana.

Ozzie also had a little red harness that Kathleen hooked up to a leash when she took him out of his case. He didn't really need it because, like Ragano and Agnes, he never left her side when they were out on the farm, preferring to stay right near his mama's feet. However, Kathleen wanted him to learn how to behave when she took him places, so they practiced every day. Ozzie got tangled quite a few times, but with some coaching from the dogs, he quickly got the hang of it. He liked being outside the best because he still had a lot of trouble walking on the slippery tile floor where his splay legs would often slide out from beneath him. Kathleen had spread throw rugs

on the kitchen floor to make it easier for him to walk, and Ozzie soon learned to stay on them as much as possible. Sometimes, however, he forgot.

Kathleen's job required her to go places to interview people for newspaper articles, and while Ragano and Agnes had to stay home, Ozzie went along in his little pink carrying case, and, unless she took him out to feed him his bottle, no one knew she was traveling with a tiny, pink piglet. He loved going for rides in the farm truck, and he even went on trips to the grocery store, his carrier slung over his mama's shoulder like a handbag, and no one knew he was there . . . except for one day . . .

Kathleen was standing in line waiting to pay for her groceries and a young boy standing behind her with his mother noticed the mesh openings on Ozzie's case. He took a peek inside.

"Hey mom!" he shouted, rather loudly for inside a store, "There's a baby pig in that bag!"

"Inside voice please," said the mother. "And there is no pig in there. Don't be ridiculous."

"But Mom!" the boy said. "There *is* a pig in there! Look!"

The mother sighed. "I'm sorry," she said to Kathleen, "but he has a very overactive imagination."

Kathleen didn't know if there were rules against bringing farm animals into grocery stores, so she whispered to the woman, "There actually is a piglet in the bag," she said, "and he's been sick so I bring him with me to keep a close eye on him. If you like, when we get outside I can take him out, and your son can meet him."

The woman's eyes grew very round. She squatted down and peeked through the mesh and smiled when she saw the tiny piglet grinning back at her.

"Why yes," she said. "I'm sure Aiden would love to meet him."

Kathleen could tell Aiden's mother wanted to meet Ozzie, as well.

Minutes later they were all outside the store and Kathleen unzipped Ozzie's bag, clipped his leash onto his harness, and lifted him out onto the sidewalk.

"I only have a few minutes," Kathleen said. "I have to get back to work."

She didn't mention she was running late because it had taken quite a while to find her truck keys, which she'd eventually located in the upstairs bathroom sink.

"I told you! I told you! I told you!" Aiden shouted, pointing at the piglet.

"My goodness," said the mother. "He's adorable!"

"He's a good boy," said Kathleen. "He always smiles, and he loves everybody."

"He's so tiny!" Aiden said.

"He was the runt, and he was very sick, but he's much better now, and he's starting to grow," Kathleen replied.

Other people had begun to gather outside the store when they realized she had a smiling little Ozzie Osboar on a leash. Kathleen grew nervous someone might step on him so she picked him up and snuggled him under her chin.

A man stepped forward and said, "You can't pick up a piglet like that. They hate it! It makes them scream!"

"I don't think so," Kathleen replied. "At least he's never screamed before."

And she lifted him up to her face and said, "Wheee piggy piggy piggy!" making Ozzie burst out in a tiny squeal of delight, then he wiggled with happiness until she did it again.

"He loves it when I pick him up," she said.

"I've raised pigs before, and I've never known one that isn't terrified to be held up like that," he said. "There must be something wrong with him."

"I don't think so," Kathleen said. "I had him checked by the veterinarian, and she said he was doing just fine. I think he just trusts me."

"Well, I hope he lives long enough for you to get some meat off of him," the man muttered, "because there's somethin' really wrong with a pig that lets you do that to him."

And he walked into the store muttering about how he knew a thing or two about pigs and that pig just wasn't right.

"You're not gonna eat him, are you?" asked Aiden.

"Absolutely not!" Kathleen gasped. "Ozzie's a pet! Nothing bad will *ever* happen to him!"

She knelt down and opened Ozzie's case to put him back inside.

"Aww," said Aiden, "can't I pet him first?"

Kathleen wanted to take her groceries and leave as quickly as possible, but the boy looked so disappointed she couldn't say no.

"Sit on the sidewalk, and I'll put him in your lap, but just for a minute," Kathleen said. "He loves it if you scratch him right between the shoulder blades."

Aiden sat down and Kathleen gently set Ozzie on his lap. Aiden carefully scratched the piglet and Ozzie giggled and stretched his nose up towards the boy.

"Oh wow," Aiden said. "Mom, can I have a baby pig? He's so cute!"

"No you may not," replied his mother. "But yes, he is adorable."

Moments later, Kathleen slipped Ozzie back into his carrier and reached for her shopping cart full of groceries. As she pushed it towards the farm truck she overheard the boy talking to his mother.

"Mom," Aiden said, "I don't want to eat bacon anymore. I like pigs better alive."

"We will talk about it when we get home," his mother replied.

Kathleen walked to the truck as quickly as she could, put the grocery bags inside, and climbed behind the steering wheel. She took Ozzie out of his case and held him close for a few minutes.

"I don't care what anyone says," she whispered. "You are the most perfect little pig that was ever born, and nothing bad will ever, ever happen to you. Your mama will take care of you, don't you worry. You are my most special little boy."

Kathleen held him up high and kissed him on the nose, and Ozzie grinned at her. He wasn't worried at all. He loved his mama, and he knew his mama loved him. Life was very good.

James, front, Falstaff behind

Chapter Six

Uncle Wilson

Falstaff stood in an unfamiliar stall and stared across the aisle at Captain. They had never spent the night away from the little barn behind the tiny farmhouse. James, the spotted appaloosa, was also in a new stall, but he was at the far end of the aisle. It had been a long time since the three of them couldn't see each other at all times, and they were very uncomfortable with the arrangement. James whinnied to his paddock mates, and both Captain and Falstaff called back to him.

"It's my fault," Falstaff said. "I bucked her off."

"It's not your fault!" Captain replied. "She deserved it!"

James whinnied again, and Falstaff and Captain whinnied back.

"What are we going to do about it?" Captain asked. "She can't get away with this. We have to find a way to tell Kathleen."

"We have to be smart about it," Falstaff said.

Captain knew he was lucky. He was a special horse that only Kathleen was allowed to handle and ride, so he didn't have to worry about Bonnie. Falstaff, however, was a jumper, and Bonnie needed a big, strong horse to take to the foxhunts and carry her over the jumps.

"Be patient," Falstaff said.

But he was worried. If he found a way to keep Bonnie from riding him, which other horses might she ride, and would she hurt them as well? There were only a few others that were big and strong enough for someone Bonnie's size. One of them was Beatrice, and she was so gentle and kind she would never understand why she was being abused. Falstaff decided he would bear the brunt of Bonnie's anger on his own. He was strong enough, at least for a while. Meanwhile, he would try to be on his best behavior; that is, until he changed his mind.

"Hi Kathleen. It's Susie Coston from Farm Sanctuary," said the voice on the other end of the phone.

"Hi Susie!" Kathleen replied. "Is everything OK?"

"Oh yes," she said. "The girls are doing fine and they're both finally healthy. I just wanted to give you an update."

"Oh good!" Kathleen said. "I've been thinking about them so much."

"I didn't tell you everything about them last time we spoke," Susie said. "I want you to know they were both so sick and traumatized from the flood that they delivered their babies way too early and none of them survived. That happened with most of the rescued sows."

"Oh, how sad," Kathleen replied.

"Yes, it was," Susie said. "I think they're depressed about it, but there was nothing we could do. They were so very sick and distressed for so long. They both had surgery at the clinic so they won't be able to have any more babies."

"I suppose that's best with all they've been through," Kathleen said. "At least they have each other. And we do have Osboar here, so maybe that will help."

Kathleen was sitting in a lawn chair in the back yard with Ragano at her feet watching Ozzie and Agnes chase each other around the Japanese maple tree. She'd already written two articles and was taking a break before returning to her computer.

"We have a date picked out for delivery if you're ready," Susie said.

"Of course!" Kathleen replied. "Any time."

Ozzie and Agnes wandered over to the paddock and stood nose-to-nose with the crabby pony, Cressida. There was chicken wire along the bottom of the fence so they couldn't get inside with the horses. Ragano trotted over to the fence and stood with the two tiny animals.

"Hi!" Ozzie said to Cressida.

Cressida stared at the piglet.

"Hi," he said again. "I'm a rock star!"

"Hmmm," Cressida replied. "I hear tell you're a baby pig. I've never seen one before you, so I have to trust what I'm told. Rock star remains to be seen."

"Everyone says I'm a pig," Ozzie replied, "but Mama says I'm her perfect little boy!" Ozzie puffed up his little chest and grinned. "I believe what my Mama tells me!"

"You might as well," Cressida said. "You'll never know the difference. At least not until the big pigs arrive."

"Big pigs?" Ozzie asked.

Ragano stepped forward.

"There are two grown-up lady pigs coming to the farm soon," Ragano said. "Do you remember your first mama?" he asked Ozzie.

"I just know the mama I have now," Ozzie said.

"Maybe because you were so sick when you were born," Ragano said, "it makes it hard to remember."

Ozzie closed his eyes for a moment and tried to think as hard as he could, but he couldn't remember any further back than the moment he looked up and saw his mama's face. She had blue eyes and a long, blonde braid, a huge smile and a bottle of warm milk in her hand. She held him close and wrapped him in soft fleece blankets and told him she loved him and would keep him safe. That was his mama.

"Nope," Ozzie said. "I only know this mama, and she tells me I'm a rock star!"

Agnes giggled, and even Cressida cracked a little smile.

Ragano only said, "Of course you're a rock star, but one day you'll realize you're also a small pig. Not a human or a puppy, but a pig. And it's good to be a pig . . . a rock star pig! Just . . . when you meet another pig, well, I hear they are going to be very, very large and they won't look at all like our Mama here on Locket's Meadow, so don't be frightened."

"I'm not frightened of anything!" Ozzie said.

And Ragano smiled at how brave the tiny piglet was, because at the very most he might have weighed two pounds.

"Ragano! Agnes! Osboar!" Kathleen called from the back door. "Time to come in! I have work to do!"

"By the way," the pony said. "In case you forgot, my name is Cressida."

"I'm Ozzie Osboar!" the piglet said. "And I'm a rock star!"

"So I've heard," Cressida said.

"Come on," Ragano said, and nudged the two smaller animals back towards the house. "Mama's calling."

Cressida wandered back over to where Locket, Classy, and Calypso were standing in the shade of the shed.

"There's something very odd about that little pig," Cressida said.

"What do you mean?" Calypso asked.

"I don't know," Cressida replied. "I think it's just . . . he's so darned happy all the time!"

The young crows were released from grounding, but they had strict instructions not to leave the farm, not even one inch over the boundaries. They weren't happy, but being out on the farm was a lot better than being confined to their tree, so they solemnly swore they would behave and flew off together to visit the little barn.

"Here comes trouble," Calypso said as the young birds swooped in and landed in a row on Locket's back. "Who let you three hoodlums out of the tree?"

But the old pony smiled as she said it, as they reminded her of their father at that age, and while he had made it very chaotic on the farm, she was quite fond of Carl.

"We are officially ungrounded," Carlyle said. "We got time off at the end for good behavior."

Carlita shuffled her feet and rather self-consciously tugged at a loose tuft of hair on Locket's back, and Cressida snickered.

"You can't fool me," Cressida said. "I know you hooligans. All that means is that you didn't get caught."

"It wasn't us!" said both boys at the same time.

All eyes turned to Carlita.

"What?" she said. "I . . . um . . . hey look!" she shouted. "Is that Uncle Wilson?"

Everyone looked to where Carlita gestured with one wing, and there, banking around the giant pine tree behind the tiny house, was a large crow. It swerved beneath the Japanese maple then up again over the barn roof before landing on Classy's back with a flourish.

"Well, Wilson, my old friend," Classy said. "We meet again."

"Uncle Wilson!" the three young crows shouted. "Yay! You're here!"

Wilson was a particularly large and handsome crow, but the horses all remembered him as a gangly pest, who, along with Carl, terrorized the farm in their youth. Carla had taken him under her wing and had done her best to keep him in line along with her son, but it was no easy task. While Carl had grown up, settled down, and built a nest for his little crows, Wilson had gone off to see the world. Every now and then he stopped home to Locket's Meadow with tales from far away lands with names like North Carolina or Canada, and the young crows would gather around and listen with rapt attention.

"Just got back in the area and thought I'd stop in and visit my favorite three little nestlings," Wilson said, "but there's nothing little about any of you anymore."

The crows beamed back at him.

"Where's your dad today?" Wilson asked.

"He and mom were cleaning up the nest," Carlita said. "Come on! They'll be so excited to see you!"

"Well, come on, little dudes and dudette." Wilson said. "Let's go find them!"

"Bye!" the crows called out and they flew back towards the big horse barn.

As they soared over the farm, Wilson asked, "So what trouble have you all been up to?"

"We're not in trouble," Carlos replied. "At least not right now. But we're teaching ourselves how to be spies!"

"Spies?" Wilson asked. "Sounds like trouble, for sure, but why?"

"Just . . . because!" Carlita said, then added, "Oh, no!"

She had spotted Bonnie leading Falstaff into the barn.

"It looks like they're going for a ride," Carlita said.

"So?" Wilson said. "That's what people do on horse farms."

"But . . . wait, I have an idea!" Carlita said. "Follow me!"

She swooped around to the east side of the barn, her brothers close behind, and flew in through the open door of the haymow. She landed on a bale of hay just above the wash stall, where the ceiling was open to the barn aisle and they could hear what was going on below.

"Why are we in here?" asked Wilson landing alongside them.

"Shhh!" said the three young crows.

"We're spying," said Carlyle.

"We'll explain later," Carlita said.

Down in the aisle Bonnie had begun to groom Falstaff. The crows peeked over the edge of the haymow floor and listened.

"We're going to the airport to meet some friends," Bonnie said. "And you *will* behave. You've been a very good boy since the last time you bucked me off and I gave you a good whipping. Turns out you're pretty stupid, but not nearly as stupid as I thought. You'll learn your lesson if I smack you hard enough!"

Wilson turned to look at the three young crows beside him, who were all horrified by what they heard. He shook his head sadly.

"Stupid, stupid horse," Bonnie said. "How pitiful your life is."

She smacked him on the leg with the brush, but Falstaff didn't flinch.

"Well, there you go," she said. "That's what I'm looking for. A well-broken horse. Really, really broken horse."

And Bonnie burst out laughing. "I guess I won, didn't I!"

"Hello!" the crows heard Kathleen's voice as she entered the barn. "Hey angel!" She said to Falstaff and kissed him on the nose. "What are you up to?"

"We're going to the airport," Bonnie said. "I have friends meeting me to trail ride."

"OK, great," Kathleen said. "Can you do me a favor and keep Captain in his stall after dinner? I may have time to ride him this evening."

"Sure," Bonnie said. "I can have him groomed for you to save you time."

"No, don't bother," Kathleen said. "I like to do it myself."

"Is that your cute little piglet in the carrier?" Bonnie asked.

"Yes, it's Osboar."

"He's just the sweetest thing," Bonnie said. "He's a lucky boy."

"I think I'm the lucky one," Kathleen said. "I'll be back in a few hours. Thank you!"

"Have a great day!" Bonnie said with a big smile.

Kathleen gave Falstaff a pat and walked past him and out the other end of the barn.

"Nothing sweet about that piglet," Bonnie muttered. "Savory is more like it."

"What does that mean?" whispered Carlita to Wilson.

"Don't worry about it," Wilson said.

"Ok, Stupid," Bonnie said. "Let's go."

She pulled the reins over Falstaff's head, gave them a yank, and led him toward the doors.

"They're leaving, but we're grounded to the farm and can't follow," Carlita said.

Wilson, who'd grown up on Locket's Meadow, knew the rules very well. Animals were to be treated kindly, and anyone who couldn't follow that simple rule wasn't welcome on the farm. Bonnie was definitely a problem, especially since she pretended to be so kind in front of Kathleen.

"You three go to the nest and tell your parents I'll be there shortly," Wilson said. "I'll follow them to the airport."

Chapter Seven

Talking up a Storm

"Mmmmma!" Ozzie said. "Mmmmmaaaaama! I can do it . . . Mmmmmmmaaaaa!"

"What are you doing?" Agnes asked.

"I'm trying to say 'Mama' out loud," Ozzie said. "You know, the way the humans talk."

Kathleen and David were both at work and the house was quiet. Ragano had moved the chairs around so Agnes could climb onto the kitchen table and be near Ozzie, who was in his guinea pig cage.

"Can pigs talk?" Aggie asked. "I thought only parrots can, like the ones in the bird room."

Kathleen had a room in the house filled with birds, many of them rescued, and many of whom could speak just like humans.

"I don't know if other pigs can talk, but I will!" Ozzie said. "I want to be able to talk to my mama and I want her to know I can say her name!"

"I wonder," Agnes asked, "why all animals can understand each other, but people can't understand us? Aren't they a kind of animal?"

Ragano was chewing on a rope toy on the floor, but he looked up and said, "I think people are too busy to listen. They run around doing so many things they don't always pay attention to what's important."

"Well, I'm gonna make Mama notice!" Ozzie said, "Because I love her best!"

"What about me?" Agnes said. "Can you love me best?"

Ozzie didn't hesitate for a moment. He smiled his happiest smile at Agnes and said, "Aggie, Mama is my most loved mama! You are my most loved best friend! I can have two most-loved because . . ."

"You're a rock star!" said both Agnes and Ragano at the same time, and all of them burst out laughing.

"You can be a rock star, too, Aggie!" Ozzie said. "Come on! Practice with me!"

"Mmmmmmmammmmma!" Ozzie said with a great deal of feeling.

Aggie tried but it came out sounding like "Oooooooowooooo!"

"That was pretty good for your first try!" Ozzie said. "Come on, try again! Mmmmmmmmmmmmmaaa!"

Aggie kept trying, but for some reason, everything she said came out sounding like a tiny, high-pitched wolf. "Oooooooooowwwwooooo!" she cried over and over. "Why can't I do this?" she asked.

"Because you're not a people," Ragano said.

"Then why don't people just learn animal speak?" Aggie sighed.

"Some can," Ragano said. "I remember when Mama didn't work so much she used to understand so much more when we talked to her."

Ever since Ozzie had arrived, all the animals had started to refer to Kathleen as Mama. The piglet may have been a tiny animal, but his enthusiasm was contagious, and within a matter of days the name-change was complete.

"So why does she have to work so much?" Ozzie asked.

"Something called 'money'," Ragano said. "It seems to be very important to them."

"Mmmmmmmmmmmmmmoneee!" Ozzie said. "Hey! I can kinda say it! It sounds a little like Mama!"

Agnes tried again, but it still sounded like "Ooooooooowoooooooooo!"

"That's OK, Aggie," Ozzie said. "Tell you what! I will do all the people talk, and maybe we can all help teach Mama how to listen to animals again. Then maybe she can forget about money and just listen to us all day."

"OK," Aggie said, "but I'm still gonna keep practicing."

And she howled like a tiny wolf while Ozzie practiced his Mmmmmaaaamaaaa sounds and Ragano occasionally took a break from chewing on his toy to look up at the pair of best friends and smile.

Wilson circled high in the sky, keeping an eye on Bonnie and Falstaff as she rode him at a walk up Old Litchfield Turnpike and onto Munson Road. The pair went up the hill, then past Verab's Nursery and to the corner by Billy's Ice Cream shop. They waited for traffic to clear, and then the two of them walked across Route 63 to the airport grounds. Wilson circled lower and lower. Several other people on horseback were waiting by the entrance to the riding trails and Bonnie waved and trotted Falstaff over to join them. Wilson circled over the woods and landed in a tree just above the riders. He could barely see them through all the leaves, but he could hear them.

"Do you think you can stay on your horse this time?" said a man's voice.

"Oh, I've got this boy whipped into shape," Bonnie replied. "He's been on good behavior. I don't think he'll ever cross me again."

"What did you do to him?" asked the man.

"Let's just say I won the battle of the wills," she replied.

Wilson scooted down lower in the branches until he could see Falstaff, who noticed him right away and gave a slight nod.

"You OK, buddy?" asked Wilson.

Falstaff stood perfectly still, but winked in Wilson's direction.

"OK, let's get going," Bonnie said.

The riders picked up their reins to turn their horses onto the bridle path, but before Bonnie could ask Falstaff to take a step he dropped his head, leaped into the air, all four feet off the ground, popped his back into a high arch and sent Bonnie flying straight up before she tumbled to the ground, landing on her butt.

Falstaff wasted no time clearing out of there. He reared on his hind legs, screamed out a deafening whinny, then turned and galloped across the fields towards the farm. Wilson stayed behind for a moment to make sure Bonnie wasn't getting up any time quickly, but she was leaning on one hip and rubbing the other, moaning, so he also took off towards the farm, catching up with Falstaff as he closed in on Route 63.

There were cars coming from the north, but Falstaff wasn't stopping to look, and Wilson swooped down and screamed, "Watch out!!" The horse stopped just in time, and as soon as the road had cleared, he took off again at a gallop, with the crow keeping pace from above. The pair turned down Old Litchfield Turnpike and Falstaff slowed to a trot.

"Fally, my man," Wilson said. "She's gonna get you for that."

"Don't care," Falstaff said. "And I will do it again when I get the chance."

"Don't blame you, dude," Wilson replied. "Where are you gonna go? Maybe go find Kathleen?"

"She won't understand," Falstaff said. "She'll think I'm misbehaving. I don't think Bonnie tells her about this, anyways."

"Someone's got to!"

Falstaff stopped in the street and Wilson landed in a branch over his head. The horse looked up at the crow.

"Who?" Falstaff said. "Who can tell her?"

The two of them said nothing more. Wilson dropped out of the branch onto Falstaff's saddle, and the two of them made their way back to the big barn.

Kathleen dropped her laptop case onto the counter as she walked into the kitchen. She was late getting home from work yet again. She took a moment to pet the dogs, then greeted Ozzie, who grinned and squealed with delight at seeing her.

To Kathleen, it sounded oddly like he had just said "Mama," but she shook her head and reached for a bottle of milk replacer to warm up for his dinner.

"Osboar, I was supposed to go ride Captain tonight, but it's so late I think all I can do is groom him and turn him back out," she said. "There just isn't enough time to do everything."

Ozzie squealed again, and Kathleen paused to stare at him.

"I don't know much about what baby pigs sound like as they grow up," she said, "but my goodness, it sounds like you're saying 'mama' when you do that!"

Ozzie grinned and squealed again, and from down on the floor Agnes began to howl. "Ooooooooooowwwwweeeeee!" she said.

"Well, I feel like I've been missed!" Kathleen said, and she picked Ozzie up and popped a nice, warm bottle into his mouth.

Kathleen walked over to the big barn on the other side of the farm. She still hadn't gotten used to Falstaff, James, and Captain not being in the little, white barn behind her house. She smiled, however, thinking about how much it had sounded like Ozzie was saying, "Mama!" when she walked in the door from work. She loved that little pig so much she could hardly believe it, and she'd been in love with animals for as long as she could remember. If only animals could really talk, she thought . . . and then she remembered that they could, and she used to hear them far more often than she did now. When had she forgotten? And when had it started?

She thought back to when she was just a little girl, no more than two-years old, and remembered the first animal she had fallen in love with. A neighbor woman, Sylvia, had a dog name Max, and she would bring him when she came to visit with Kathleen's mother in the backyard. The huge German shepherd had fascinated Kathleen, and she stared at him as he curled up obediently near his mama's feet. Her mother and Sylvia had warned her that Max didn't like small children and would bite her, but Kathleen didn't care. She crept closer. She remembered talking to the dog, but inside her head, not out loud.

"I want to pet you," she said.

And the dog responded inside her head.

"If you pet me, I will bite you," Max said.

"I don't care," she had replied.

"Then go ahead," Max said.

Kathleen hadn't thought twice about it, it was so important to her that she touched the long, black coat of the gigantic dog. She crept closer, and when her mother and Sylvia weren't paying attention, she reached over and gently ran her hand down Max's back. Max growled and nipped her arm.

"That's OK," she said to Max in her head, and she looked at the teeth marks in her skin, more out of curiosity than anything else.

Her mother and Sylvia turned when they heard Max growl, and Kathleen didn't remember anything after that other than voices yelling at Max for biting, then at Kathleen for going near the dog. She was whisked into the house where her mother scrubbed the bite and dabbed orange medicine on it, and Sylvia took Max home, but Kathleen didn't cry. She didn't care that he'd bitten her. She was pleased she'd touched the handsome dog. It wasn't the last time she would pet him, and it wasn't the last time he would bite her arm, but she never cared, and never cried, and always enjoyed her short conversations with him. She remembered three bites before Sylvia stopped bringing Max to the house, and then she missed him terribly.

There were many other times she'd clearly heard animals speak to her, especially when she was a child, but few stuck with her as strongly as the soft, deep voice of Max; they understood each other. The only people who didn't understand were the grown-ups, and now that Kathleen was a grown-up, the voices were few and far between. What happened, she wondered? Did growing up mean all the magic had to go away?

She entered the big barn and her horses whinnied in greeting.

"Hello, my angels!" she said and patted each one on the nose as she worked her way down to Captain's stall. She stopped in front of him and he tilted his head and smiled, then leaned forward to give his mama a kiss. He was a very special horse, and they had grown incredibly close since he'd arrived four years earlier.

"My handsome man," she said. "I don't have time to ride tonight, but I can give you a good grooming. I'm so sorry."

Kathleen lifted his purple halter from his door and went into his stall. Captain put his head on her shoulder and tilted it so it leaned into the crook of her neck. Kathleen felt a tear run down her cheek.

"Why don't I ever have any time anymore?" she said, and wrapped her arms around his neck to give him a hug. "Tomorrow I have a huge deadline and I have to go in to work early to start."

She turned her face into Captain's neck to wipe the tear onto his shiny coat. "I'm so sorry," she said.

"It's OK, Mama," she heard in her head.

"No," she answered before she even realized what had just happened. "No, it's not OK!"

And then she paused and took a step back, staring hard into the big, brown eyes of her handsome horse.

Chapter Eight

Bird Brains

When a baby pig isn't raised with other pigs, he has no way of understanding what his own species is. All the talk about the new pigs arriving meant nothing to Ozzie. He had his mama, his friends Ragano and Agnes, the many house cats, the parrots in the bird room and the horses at the fence line. Ozzie learned how to rumble with the dogs, how to pounce with the cats, and he even practiced waddling behind the big goose, Percival. So why not practice talking like a human? Especially when one is convinced he really is a rock star. Every day was a new opportunity for Ozzie Osboar to play, snuggle, nap, and drink warm milk. Why worry about tomorrow when today was so pleasant?

By the time Ozzie was three-weeks old he had more than tripled in size and Kathleen had to move him from the table to the kitchen floor and give him a dog crate to stay in when she was out of the house. His back legs still slid down flat to the floor when he tried to walk on the slippery tile, but as long as he remembered to walk on the rugs he did just fine.

It was the first week of September, and the tomatoes were still ripening thick and fast in the garden. Many evenings, Ozzie followed his mama as she walked around the kitchen making pot after pot of tomato sauce and pouring it into big jars. Sometimes she'd open a jar of the applesauce she'd made the previous fall and put a tiny bit on a saucer for Ozzie to lick up. He was starting to eat a little bit of soft food, like cooked carrots and mashed bananas, but applesauce was the most delicious food in the world, aside from warm milk, of course.

"No, no, Ozzie!" Mama said when he came too close while Kathleen was carrying hot pots and jars "No, no! You stay back! You don't want to get hurt!"

"No, no," seemed like a useful pair of words to Ozzie once he understood the meaning of them, and he added it to his human talking practice sessions that he held with Ragano and Agnes while Mama was at the office. He decided to save up as many human words as he could and surprise her one day.

On nice days Kathleen sat at the picnic table in the back yard, typing the day's articles, while Ozzie, Agnes, and Ragano romped in the grass, racing up the hill through the wildflower garden packed with black-eyed Susans and down and around the Japanese maple, over and over again. When they grew tired, they'd flop down in the shade beneath the deep red leaves and talk about everything and nothing, then doze in a big pile of pig and puppies.

Sometimes Ozzie practiced his words. He could say "mama" quite well, but he was struggling with his "no, no."

"Nuh, huh," he would say over and over again. "Nuh! Nuh! I'm gonna get this!"

"Of course you will," Agnes said.

She had given up on trying to talk human. No matter what she did, everything came out sounding like, "Ooooooooooowooooo!"

One day, while lying beneath the maple tree, Ozzie spied three tiny pairs of black eyes staring at him through the leaves. He stared right back.

"Hello!" he said. "How are you?"

"Oh, man!" a discouraged voice answered. "He saw us!"

"We got too close," a second voice answered.

"Yea, Uncle Wilson warned us about that," said a third voice.

Ragano lifted his head from his nap.

"Hello Carlyle, Carlos, and Carlita," he said. He knew the young crows quite well, and had heard all the stories told about their father's adventures growing up on the farm. "What are you up to?"

The three birds flapped down to the lowest branches of the wide tree so they were nearly eye-level with Ragano.

"We're practicing our spying," Carlita said. "We want to be spies, but it's harder than we thought."

"What's spying?" Ozzie asked.

"It's when you watch someone but they don't know you're watching them," Carlos said.

"And then you report back to home base with information," Carlyle said.

"What's a home base?" Ozzie asked, although he was more confused about why anyone would want to watch someone and not be discovered. He was happy to talk to anyone at anytime, so hiding made no sense to him.

"Well, we don't have a home base yet," Carlita said. "We haven't gotten that far."

"Is this a game you're playing?" Agnes asked.

"No!" Carlita answered. "It's serious business! We have a problem on the farm, and we have to help find a way to fix it!"

"Bonnie and Falstaff?" Ragano asked.

"How do you know?" the three crows asked in unison.

"Locket told me everything," Ragano replied.

Ozzie and Agnes looked at him, confused.

"I didn't tell you because I don't want you to worry," Ragano said. "Falstaff can take care of himself . . . for now."

Ragano knew his job well, and it was to protect the farm. He had decided his two very young charges should be protected from knowing something bad was happening.

"Bonnie pretends to be nice when Kathleen is around, but when she's not, she's really mean to Falstaff," Carlita said. "She *hits* him!"

"What's that mean?" Ozzie asked.

"Nothing you ever have to worry about," Ragano said.

"So Uncle Wilson was here," Carlita said, "and he saw what Bonnie was doing to Falstaff, and he followed them up to the airport and saw Falstaff buck her off and run back home, and then we hid in the haymow and watched when Bonnie got back and she took her boot off and started hitting him with it!"

"And Falstaff stood there and didn't move," Carlyle said. "Not one tiny bit."

"I would have bit her or kicked her, but he just stood perfectly still," Carlos said. "I don't know why!"

"So we went back to the tree, and Wilson told Mom and Dad, which was good because that meant I didn't have to do it so I didn't get into trouble for leaving the nest when I was grounded," Carlita said. "Oops . . . I didn't mean to say that."

"And then Mom and Dad said it was OK if we wanted to be spies!" Carlos said. "Well, Dad said it was OK. Mom wasn't very happy about it."

"And if we had to go someplace to spy on account of Falstaff, we're allowed to leave the farm again!" Carlyle said. "But only for Falstaff, because if it's for anything else, they'll send us to Grandmother for punishment."

The three young crows shuddered.

"What do you think you can do to help him?" Agnes asked.

The crows were quiet.

"We don't know yet," Carlita finally said. "But we have to do something!"

"Did you talk to Falstaff?" Ragano asked.

"Yes, and he said he could take care of himself," Carlos said.

"But Bonnie is still being mean to him," Carlyle said, "and nobody knows why!"

"Be careful, little buddies," Ragano said. "You don't want to get caught. And if you find out anything, what are you going to do with it?"

"We don't know," Carlita said. "Nobody knows how to tell Kathleen what Bonnie's really like."

"I can do it!" Ozzie said. "I'm teaching myself how to talk human!"

"You can talk human?" Carlita asked.

"Listen!" Ozzie answered, practically dancing with excitement. "Mama! Mama Mama! And I'm learning, 'Nuh! Nuh!'"

"He's saying 'no, no,'" Agnes said. "I keep trying but it just sounds like, 'ooooowoooooo!'"

"Hey, I wonder if I can talk human!" Carlita said. "I've never thought about trying."

"The birds inside the house all talk human," Ozzie said. "I only know 'mama' and 'nuh,' so far. But I think I can learn more!"

"Hmmm," Carlita said, then opened her beak and tried to make the sound of "mama," and what came out was surprisingly close. "Hey, I almost did it!"

The boys tried, as well, and they also made similar noises.

Ozzie raced in a small circle, joining them.

"We can talk human!" he cried. "We can talk human!"

Kathleen looked up from her laptop. She thought she'd heard a chorus of very young children calling out for their mama, but all she saw was Ozzie, Ragano and Agnes beneath the spreading maple, and a handful of crows sitting on a low branch.

"What are you guys up to?" Kathleen called out.

The crows took off flying, and the piglet and dogs came running to her.

"Come on in," Kathleen said, standing up and closing her laptop. "Let's get lunch before I head to the office."

The three young crows flew back towards the big barn and landed on a fence rail between two paddocks. On one side of the fence stood

Captain, Falstaff, and James, and on the other side stood two more of the early rescues, Ernie and Star. Ernie was a Shire, the biggest horse on the farm, a dark bay color with three white socks. Star was a half-Belgian draft and a big horse, as well, but Ernie was so big he made Star look small. The two had lived together from shortly after being rescued.

"We can talk human!" Carlyle said. "Mamamamamama!"

Carlita rolled her round black eyes. "You know one word," she said. "Big deal. I think there are a few more than that."

"But we really do know one word!" Carlos shouted, and he and his brother both chanted together, "Mama! Mama! Mama! Mama!"

The horses lifted their heads from their lunch hay.

"Did they just talk human?" James asked.

"Sure sounded like it," Falstaff said.

All five horses walked over to the crows.

"How are you doing that?" asked Ernie.

"Ozzie is teaching himself how to talk human!" Carlita said. "And we just learned it from him!"

"Agnes is trying to learn, too, but she can't do it," Carlos said.

"But we tried it and it's easy!" Carlyle said.

Captain and Falstaff looked at each other and they each knew they were thinking the same thing. Could the crows help them find a way to tell Kathleen about Bonnie? And if so, how? Learning new human words wouldn't be easy. When animals talk to each other, and they all can, it's not the same way people do it. They connect with each other in their minds, and they understand each other perfectly without having to use the same kind of language that humans need. Their language is built into their souls, and they're born knowing it. They understand what people say when they talk to animals because, even when they're using human words, their meaning is also in their minds. While horses and dogs will learn to understand lots and lots of human words and what they mean, like "cookie" and "stay," they can't say them the same way, not with their mouths or their heads. So the problem was, where could the crows learn more human words when there weren't any talking animals to teach them?

"The bird room!" Captain said. "The parrots can talk! They can teach them more words!"

"Guys," Falstaff said to the crows, "can you keep your talking a secret? We think we know a way you can help us get rid of Bonnie, but no one can find out what you know how to do."

Locket's Meadow was filled with very special animals, and Captain was one of the most special of all. When he'd first arrived on the farm as an angry colt, he struck out at any humans who dared come near him . . . except for Kathleen. Somehow, Kathleen had known his name, the one his mother had given him, and for that he had loved her right from the start. With a lot of patience and love from his new mama, he'd grown into a handsome, wise, and caring horse. While Locket had the gift of being able to talk to spirits and animals that were far away, Captain's gift was knowing lots of things about people and animals that no one had ever told him. He could look at anyone and know their heart, their dreams, and even what they'd had for breakfast that morning. Like Calypso, he had known Bonnie was a bad person right from the start. Yet even he couldn't have guessed at her cruelty.

Captain knew Kathleen's heart better than anyone, and they were so close that when he and his mama went riding, all she had to do was think about what she wanted from Captain, and he did it. He could read her every thought, and he knew that sometimes she could read his. Why, then, couldn't she hear him all the time? He'd be able to tell her about how horribly Bonnie treated Falstaff. If she knew, she would definitely make Bonnie go away.

That evening, as Captain stood in his stall in the big barn that was still so strange to him, he tried to remember each time he'd known his mama had heard him talking to her, hoping he could figure how to make it happen again. He knew she'd heard him just a few days ago when she came to groom him and was sad. What was the secret? How did he make her understand? And then . . . he "felt" her walking towards the barn. He saw the other horses leaning out of their stalls to see, and heard the chorus of whinnies when they recognized who it was.

"Hey angel horse," Kathleen said when she got to his stall. "I'm late again. I'm so sorry."

She reached into her pocket and took out a peppermint and fed it to him. He tilted his head up and smiled at her.

"The whole rest of the week is going to be like this," she said. "Maybe next week will be better."

Kathleen stepped into his stall and reached up to wrap her arms around his neck, but he took a step backwards.

"Oh no. Are you mad at me?" she asked.

Captain snorted high into the air, then leaned in close to her face and stared hard into her eyes.

"What's the matter?" Kathleen asked, confused.

Captain breathed hard, directly into her face, but she didn't flinch. She trusted her horse to be careful with her. Moments went

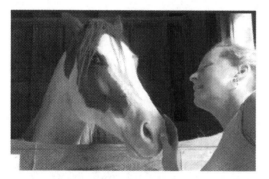

by before she realized he wanted her to breathe back at him, the way horses sometimes did in the field, back and forth into each other's nostrils. She tilted her head back and breathed, then closed her eyes. In her mind she could see

Captain and Mama

herds of horses racing across huge, grassy fields beneath a cloudless blue sky. A brown and white paint stallion reared high and pawed at the air and a group of foals hung back with their mamas. She could smell the horses and the trampled grass, almost feel the sun on her face . . . and then Captain stopped. The vision disappeared, and she opened her eyes and took a step back.

"What was that about, handsome man?" she asked.

But Captain just leaned his head on her shoulder, and his mama reached up and wrapped her arms around his neck.

Harriet and Ice

Chapter Nine

The Sisters

"Sister," Harriet said, "where exactly did they say we are going?"

"They didn't," Ice replied. "I haven't a clue what's in store for us next."

"I hope there are no cages, wherever 'next' may be," Harriet said. "I couldn't bear to go back into a cage after all this, dear Sister. Stalls are so much nicer. And cleaner!"

Earlier that morning, after a light breakfast, the sisters had been escorted from their stall and herded down the aisle to where a trailer had backed up to the big double doors. They were very suspicious of the metal ramp, and both hesitated to walk up it despite the piles of soft bedding that awaited them. The humans, however, insisted, and nudged against their rumps when they hesitated.

Harriet resisted as long as she could. She was concerned about the smooth, metal ramp as the infection in her foot had been so deep the veterinarians had to remove one of her toes, and she was still unsteady. With enough gentle pushing from behind and a few apples to lure them through the doorway, the ladies finally relented and scurried into the trailer. The doors quickly closed behind them, the truck engine started, and the trailer jiggled its way down the driveway. Neither of the sisters spoke a word, but each knew what the other was deathly afraid of . . . returning to the cages. The stall had given them room to stand up, stretch and walk around, even if only in circles. It was cleaned every day, at least twice. There was no manure or urine beneath them to burn their skin or make them dirty and smelly. And while it was sometimes noisy when workers brought food to the animals, it never matched the noise of their previous barn filled with hundreds of bored, angry and sore pigs. The stall at the vet clinic had been heaven-on-earth to the pair of pigs from Iowa.

Also, neither of the sisters mentioned their late-night conversations with the burro from Locket's Meadow. With all they'd been through, they'd had enough bad luck to know their good luck might be temporary. Heaven only knew what was next for the ladies! But they were together, whatever happened, which was the most important thing. They could handle anything if they stayed side-by-side. They settled into the clean pile of straw, resigned to how little control they had over their lives.

At six-weeks old, Ozzie Osboar was growing faster and faster. He was getting so heavy that if he walked off the rugs and onto the kitchen tile and his legs slipped out from beneath him, it grew harder and harder for him to stand up again.

When he was outside, however, the soft ground, grass and rough sidewalks were safe for his tricky splay legs. He liked playing in the back yard with the dogs, but he also loved the side yard where the ducks and the giant goose, Percival, lived. The side yard had a white picket fence surrounding gardens and a tiny duck pond with two little waterfalls and lots of flowers and grass. Mama let him out there by himself because she could watch him from the window over the kitchen sink or the one next to her desk in her office.

Kathleen had read it was easy to train pigs, and Ozzie had potty trained very quickly, but because of his splay legs there were some things he couldn't do. His legs weren't built for sitting the way the dogs did, but if his mama gently patted him on the back he would lie down on his tummy. Then she patted him again to ask him to roll over onto his side so she could rub his belly. He'd also learned to walk on his leash and stayed at Kathleen's heel, just like the dogs did.

Ozzie was now so big that when it was time for his bottle his mama would call him and he'd come running and drink down all his milk in less than two minutes before running back out to play. He also ate small dishes of soft food several times a day. He was so big that when Mama picked him up and held him high over her head, singing, "Wheee! Piggy! Piggy! Piggy!" she would set him back down and sigh, then say, "Osboar, you're growing so quickly I don't know how much longer I can keep doing that." Then, she would pick him up high over her head again so he would squeal with delight, because she knew that one day, no matter how strong she was, her little pig would grow way too heavy for their favorite game.

Ozzie had grown much larger than Agnes, but of course, Agnes was a Jack Rat Terrier, which is a very small breed of dog. The size difference didn't stop the best friends from playing for hours and hours in the back yard, while Ragano watched closely to make sure everyone stayed safe. Ozzie spent so much time with the dogs that he'd even learned how to bark, and when visitors arrived he'd run to the gate with Agnes and Ragano, barking at the top of his lungs.

It was late afternoon on a mild September day. It still felt like summer even though the sun slanted through the trees much lower in the sky, reminding the residents of the farm, both animal and human, that the days were getting shorter and winter wasn't far away. Ozzie and the dogs had stopped playing to rest beneath the Japanese maple, which was turning from deep red to green, as that kind of tree does in defiance of the way most every other tree approaches autumn. Ozzie was stretched out on his side, dozing, when he heard wings flapping overhead and recognized the sound of crows landing in the tree above him. He rolled onto his stomach, yawned and looked up.

"I hope you weren't practicing your spying today," Ozzie said, "because that was a pretty loud landing!"

"Nope!" said Carlita. "We're here on official business!"

"Official?" said Ragano. "Sounds important!"

"It is!" Carlos said. "We need to learn more human words!"

"Lots and lots of them!" Carlyle added.

"And Falstaff and Captain think we should find the cage birds and ask them to teach us some," Carlita said.

"You'll have to ask Mama to let you in the house," Ozzie said. "Do you know enough human talk to do that?"

"I don't think 'nuh Mama' is going to help them much with that," Agnes said.

"And it won't be very spy-like, either," said Carlita.

"Where are these birds?" Carlos asked.

"In the bird room," Ozzie said. "Follow me!"

Agnes and Ragano scrambled to their feet and followed Ozzie, while the crows flapped right behind him. He trotted around to the side of the house where there was a row of windows that gave the inside birds lots of light. In the summer, the windows were usually closed to keep the air conditioning in, and of course they were closed in the winter against the cold, but sometimes, in the spring and fall, the windows were open a few inches to let fresh air inside. Today was just such a day, and they were cracked open near the bottom, so the piglet, dogs and crows lined up and peered inside.

"Hello!" Ozzie said. "Anyone awake?"

The room had seven large cages in it, each one with one parrot inside. Ozzie had gotten very friendly with the birds, especially the African Grey named Polonius. Polonius was a very smart and dignified bird who had taken a liking to the little pig and often tossed tiny pieces of bird kibble to the floor for Ozzie to eat.

"Polonius!" he called again.

"My goodness!" Polonius said, shaking out her feathers. "It's pre-dinner nap time, Ozzie!" she said. "You know better!"

"But Polonius," Ozzie replied, "there are birds here who want to learn how to speak human like you do. These crows!" Ozzie nodded in their direction.

"Crows!" Polonius said. "Crows speaking human? I've never heard of that. Humans speak human. Parrots speak human. Crows? You aren't even hook bills!" she added. "I don't think it's possible!"

"But they can!" Ozzie said. "I taught them how to say 'mama!'"

The three crows immediately erupted into a huge chorus of "mamamamamama!"

"Shhhhh!" Polonius said. "I believe you! But you'll wake up the entire room. Why on earth do you want to learn human?"

"Because we are *spies!*" whispered Carlita.

"Wait a minute," Polonius said. "Are you Carla's grandchildren?"

"Yes!" they all replied.

"Hmmmmm," the parrot said. "I know a select group of words that may or may not help you with spying."

"Teach us!" the crows chanted.

"I don't usually dally with outside birds," Polonius said, "but I have a great admiration for your grandmother. I suppose I can teach you a few things, but we have to be quick. Mama will close the windows soon since it gets cold at night. Let's start with some phrases I've often heard spoken in the house. Are you ready?"

"Yes!" the crows said.

"Here's a popular one that I heard often when Agnes was younger," Polonius said. "Are you ready?"

The three crows nodded, eager to begin.

"All right then," Polonius said. "Repeat after me. 'No, no, bad dog! Don't poop on my floor. Go outside!'"

Agnes dropped to her belly and tucked her face beneath her paw. "Do you have to teach them that?" she asked.

"I believe it will be most useful if I teach them some of the human's most frequently used phrases," Polonius answered. "So floor poop it is! Now repeat!"

The crows chanted after Polonius, over and over, each time getting slightly better, until Polonius decided they were close enough for their first try.

"Alright!" she said. "Let's try one more for today. . ."

But before she could say anything else, her voice was drowned out by the noise of a diesel pickup truck pulling a trailer. It drove slowly past the house, then turned and climbed up the sloping driveway.

"Who is that?" Ragano asked and he and Agnes raced around to the back of the house, barking furiously.

"Guess I gotta go," Ozzie said, "See ya later!"

He turned and raced after the dogs, barking, "Woof! Woof! Woof!" as he caught up with them at the gate.

Harriet and Ice felt the trailer climb a short, bumpy hill and braced themselves so they didn't tip over. Moments later, when the truck stopped, the only sound the pigs could hear was barking dogs – lots of them.

"Dogs," said Harriet, who remembered them from her days in the crate; sometimes dogs had followed The Men into the big barns where they'd lived in their cages.

"Dogs!" said Ice. "No! They had dogs at the cages! No! No! NO!" she cried.

"Shhh," Harriet said. "Sister, do not panic. If it is a place of cages we will plot our escape, sooner rather than later. We will watch for an opening as soon as they open the back of this container and let us out. Do you understand?"

Ice nodded. She couldn't speak, she was so afraid she'd be forced back into another cold, hard prison.

"And remember, dearest sister," Harriet said. "We stay together *no matter what*!"

The sisters backed as far as they could into a corner of the trailer and waited.

Cressida

Chapter Ten

Are We Home Yet?

"They're here!" Kathleen shouted when she heard the trailer grinding over the gravel driveway. She'd been scrubbing dog and pig nose prints off the bottom kitchen cabinet doors, but she tossed her sponge into the sink and raced to the back door to call the dogs and Ozzie into the house. They were in the backyard and all three were barking so frantically that Kathleen decided to leave them there; they would never hear her calling over their own noise. She stuffed her feet into her work boots and went outside to greet the two drivers from Farm Sanctuary who were delivering the two newest additions to the farm.

"Hi!" Kathleen said, shaking their hands. "I'm Kathleen. If you back the trailer right up to that barn door, we can unload the girls out there. We're keeping them in a stall tonight so they can get settled and we'll move them to a paddock in the morning."

The drivers backed the trailer up to the north side of the barn, and everyone gathered in the aisle to help guide the sisters to where they'd stay on their first night in their new home. The horses were in their stalls finishing their dinner, and Cressida, Locket, and Classy peered over the tops of their doors on one side of the aisle while Calypso and the goats watched from the other. A group of noisy crows hopped about in the branches of the maple tree alongside the barn door and the dogs and Ozzie made a ruckus in the yard.

"You be quiet, dogs!" Kathleen shouted from the barn, but they only hesitated for a moment. "I'll bring them in the house as soon as we're done unloading. The girls had a long ride. I want to get them settled as quickly as possible."

She closed up the doors at the other end of the barn to cut down on the level of dog noise, but it didn't help very much.

The drivers opened the trailer doors and lowered the ramp, and everyone peered inside, anxious to meet the new residents.

"Come on, angels!" Kathleen said. "You can come out, now!"

The two sows were pressed firmly together, eying the humans. The dogs suddenly grew quiet, and moments later, David entered the barn.

"Sorry," he said. "I couldn't get out here any faster. The dogs and Ozzie were so excited they weren't listening to me, and I had to put them on leashes to make them go inside. Well, look at them!" he said as he spotted the pigs on the trailer. "Those are some big girls!"

The horses craned their necks further forward, trying to see.

"I brought apples," David said, and he and Kathleen each took one and walked up the ramp towards the sister.

"Come on, pretty girls," Kathleen said. "We have lots of fresh bedding and clean water all ready for you."

The sisters sniffed the apples, then slowly, still pressed tightly together, carefully walked down the ramp and stopped at the bottom.

"This way," Kathleen said, backing into an open stall. "Right here, angels."

The ladies slowly followed the couple into the stall. They each gently took an apple, and then David and Kathleen left the stall and slid the door closed.

"That wasn't so bad," David said.

"Poor things look so scared," Kathleen said. "I assume we have paperwork to sign?" she asked the drivers.

Later, when the humans had left the barn, the two new pigs walked to their door, a sliding metal grate that was easy to see through.

"Sister!" said Harriet. "It's a stall! No cages! No cages!"

"No cages," said Ice. "It's clean. It's clean!"

Ice picked up a snout-full of shavings and tossed them in the air.

"Clean shavings!" Ice said again. "No cages!

Locket tilted her head at the two newest residents of the farm.

"Hello," she said. "I'm Locket. Welcome to Locket's Meadow."

It was much later that night before Kathleen finally got to bed. She and David had gone back out to the barn with a flashlight to check on Harriet and Ice. When they peeked into the stall they were surprised to find a huge pile of perfectly mounded straw and two pink noses poking out, side-by-side. The sisters were sound asleep.

"Oh how sweet!" Kathleen said. "They made themselves a little nest!"

"Little?" said David. "There's nothing little about those girls or their nest. They must be at least six hundred pounds each!"

"Let's let them sleep," Kathleen said. "We can get to know them better in the morning."

They stared at the pair of noses for a few more minutes before leaving the barn and closing it up for the night.

Kathleen opened her laptop on the kitchen table. She couldn't stop thinking about how terrified Harriet and Ice were as they inched their way off the trailer. She knew how horrible factory farming was for other animals, but until the arrival of Ozzie Osboar, she knew little about pigs, and the truth was, she hadn't thought about them at all. Why not, she wondered?

For the past six years she and David had been taking care of animals

Doc, front, Calypso, behind

that had arrived from every horrible situation imaginable. Some were intercepted on their way to slaughter; others had been abandoned, while still others had been abused. They had roosters rescued from cock fighting and ducks that were abandoned on ponds when families grew tired of them after Easter. All of them, Kathleen thought, were victims of bullying by human beings. Her job as their caretaker was to never allow any of them to be bullied again. She needed to learn why their two new ladies were so frightened.

She opened her laptop and typed in "factory farming pigs."

The residents of the little barn, aside from the goats who stayed inside after dark, were out in their paddock for the night. It was another cool September evening, and the moon was a silver sliver in the western sky. They stood quietly, thinking about what they'd just learned from Harriet and Ice. The ladies had told them tales of cages, electrified sticks for poking to make them move along, babies being snatched away from mamas, babies they had never had a chance to properly take care of or love. They told them about the rising floods and how they'd escaped together and swam to the levee. They told how other pigs were being shot and killed around them, and how they crouched behind the bodies of the dead to stay alive. And then they told them about their many weeks in the hospital, so sick they almost died.

Finally Classy spoke.

"We hear so many stories from the animals that come here," she said. "Terrible, terrible stories. We sometimes don't realize how lucky we are that we're safe."

"We *are* the lucky ones," Cressida said. "Aside from Locket, the rest of us weren't rescued from anyplace. We were just ordinary animals. We never knew about any of these terrible things. I feel guilty for being so crabby. My problems seem small, now."

"I have never been so grateful to just be an old lesson pony," Calypso said.

"I have a confession," Locket said.

The others turned to her.

"I spoke with Harriet and Ice weeks ago," she said. "I didn't tell you about it because it was before Ozzie even got here, and I didn't know if the sisters would ever find us. I didn't even know what a baby pig looked like, never mind a grown pig!"

"Why didn't you say anything?" Classy asked. She looked a little hurt – the two of them always told each other everything.

"I don't know," Locket said. "I guess it just seemed so . . . impossible that they'd get here. We didn't have pigs then."

"It's Locket's Meadow," Calypso said. "Nothing is impossible here."

"I know," Locket said. "I'm sorry."

"It doesn't matter," Classy said. "They found us and they're safe. They won't ever have to deal with abuse again."

"Unless Bonnie gets at them," Cressida said.

They all fell silent. They felt terrible for everything the pigs had suffered through, but there was still a bully right there on their own farm, and so far no one had figured out how to save Falstaff from her.

Kathleen closed her laptop – she'd done enough research for one night. She knelt down on the floor where Ozzie was curled up under a light fleece blanket; she loved how he always seemed to be smiling, even in his sleep. She gently tucked the edges of the blanket around him and he sighed deeply.

"Nobody is ever going to hurt you," she said. "Your mama will always take care of you."

She went upstairs and found David reading in bed.

"I thought the flooding in Iowa was the worst thing in the world," she said. "But I just learned so much more."

David sighed and closed his book.

"What did you find out?" he asked.

"OK, first, mama pigs are put into crates as soon as they're pregnant with their first litter and they spent their entire pregnancy there – not just part of it," Kathleen said. "These crates are so small they can't move at all. And then . . . a few days before they deliver they're moved to the gestation crates which are slightly bigger so they can lie on their sides so their babies can nurse. But get this! When the babies are born they never have a chance to clean them up and take care of them. The mamas are completely trapped! The piglets nurse through the bars of a cage and the mothers can't mother them. Then - the babies are taken away at three-weeks old and packed into crowded sheds to fatten for slaughter. The mothers are moved back to gestation crates and artificially inseminated, and it starts all over again. This goes on for several years, and then the mothers are slaughtered. What kind of crazy people think of such things? Human beings are horrible!"

"Not all of them," David said. "You aren't. We aren't."

"I think I'm most upset because for all this time I've worried about rescuing horses," she said, "and so many of them have terrible lives and they deserve better, but almost all pigs live horrible, hopeless, painful lives. And I didn't pay attention, at least not until Osboar. And," she added, with tears running down her cheeks, "he's so special, and so perfect. If we hadn't gotten him . . ."

"If we hadn't gotten him he wouldn't have lived long enough to suffer through any of it," David interrupted her. "You kept him alive."

"What do we do?" Kathleen said.

"We do what we've been doing," David said. "We help the ones we can."

"That's not enough," Kathleen replied.

Harriet and Ice

Chapter Eleven

Words of Wisdom

At the very rear of the yard where Ozzie and the dogs played beneath the Japanese maple tree there was a long, narrow, grassy paddock that stretched all the way back to the woods. Just inside the gate stood a shed that was plenty big enough for two very large sows, and that would be the sisters' new home. The next morning, as the sun was rising, Kathleen and David went outside with a small bucket of apples to move them to their new space. The sisters were awake and walking in circles in their stall.

"Come on, ladies," Kathleen said. "It's time!"

Kathleen slid the stall door open, and David shook the bucket of apples. The girls pressed themselves together and slowly left the stall, following the couple as they walked backwards up the hill to the fence. The sows followed them through the gate, then David poured the apples into feeding dishes near the shed door. Then the pair of humans slipped out through the gate.

"I want to watch for a few minutes," Kathleen said. "They've never been outside like this. I'll come help feed in a little while."

"Take your time," David said.

"Sister," Harriet said when she'd finished her apples. "There is no roof! We can see the sky!"

"Yes sister," Ice said. "We are free, you and I. I am so happy I could cry!"

"Look, sister!" Harriet said, "I can fly!"

She kicked up her heels, and despite having only half of her back right foot, she raced through the green grass and wildflowers to the very back of their new yard.

"I'm right behind you!" Ice said, and she followed her to the back fence, where they both turned around and ran right back to the front again.

"My goodness!" Harriet said. "Who knew running could be so exhilarating?"

Ice poked her nose into the soil and rooted around. "I think I smell something delicious," she said, digging some more. "Oh my . . . oh my!"

Harriet trotted into the deep grass and nibbled on the tips that had gone to seed. It was beyond delicious. She had never been outside before aside from when they'd escaped from the flooding, and then, they were only focused on swimming and staying alive.

"Look, Sister!" Ice cried out. "There's straw in the shed for bedding! I shall do our housekeeping!"

She grabbed big mouthfuls of straw and shook it, fluffing it up to make their bed. Harriet trotted over and joined her.

"Do you think this is real?" Harriet asked. "Do you think we are safe?"

"One day at a time, dear sister," Ice said. "We must appreciate it while it lasts. And we must be strong!"

"So it lasts long," Harriet said, and the two of them set about to fluffing their bedding and turning their little paddock into their new home, for however long it would last . . .

Falstaff, Captain, and James huddled over the breakfast hay in their paddock. It had been several days since the new pigs arrived, and the farm was still buzzing about the latest rescue. The mood in the boy's paddock, however, was quite grim, as the battle between Falstaff and Bonnie had escalated over the past few weeks.

"How long do you think you can stand this?" Captain asked.

"As long as I have to," Falstaff said.

"It just gets worse," Captain said. "She gets meaner, you throw her to the ground, then she gets meaner again. Sooner or later one of you is going to crack. Or get seriously hurt."

James looked up from his hay. He was a very quiet, mild-mannered horse, but beneath that, he was always thinking. Quiet thoughts, of course, but lots of them.

"Did you have an idea, James?" Falstaff asked.

"I'm still thinking," James replied.

"I'm still trying to make Kathleen hear me," Captain said. "Sometimes she does, but it's not easy when she's always thinking about so many other things. And even when she hears me she doesn't listen long enough."

"The crows are working on their human talk," Falstaff said. "I'm not sure how useful it is. Yesterday they said they learned how to say, 'lie down and stay,' and 'be quiet! Nobody wants to listen to your barking all day.'"

James glanced up and smiled.

Captain rolled his eyes. "You never know when phrases like that will come in handy," he said. "Why can't she teach them something like, "Bonnie's a two-faced, crazy, mean, horse-beating . . ."

"Easy, buddy," Falstaff interrupted him. "They're doing their best. Still thinking, James?"

"Yep," James replied and reached for another bite of hay.

"I can only hold back for so long before I buck her off," Falstaff said. "But I try to let her have a few good rides in between because I want to be the only one she rides. What if she hurts one of the others? Beatrice, Ernie, Star . . . they're the right size for her to ride, and they can jump fences. If she gets mad at them . . . yesterday she threw water buckets at my legs when she got back from the airport."

"Did she hurt you?" Captain asked.

"No," Falstaff replied.

"But she could have," James said.

"Don't worry, she didn't," Falstaff said.

"But she could have," James said again.

"But . . ." Falstaff said.

"And then you would have a sore leg, and you would have to limp," James said.

"But . . ." Falstaff said again, "but . . . but James, you're right. She really could have hurt me. And I *would* have to limp."

"Yep," said James, and he smiled and reached down for another bite of hay.

Captain looked from James to Falstaff and back again. And then his eyes lit up, as he understood the plan.

Ozzie had not yet met the sister pigs. His mama had taken him up the hill to introduce him, but the ladies were sunbathing at the back of their paddock, and neither one budged an inch when they were called. The tops of their pink backs were just visible over the white Queen Anne's lace and pink coneflowers.

"That's OK, Osboar," Kathleen said. "You'll have plenty of time to get to know them. We'll just let them relax and soak up the sun. They seem so happy!"

Ozzie still hadn't gotten a good look at them. Whenever he was outside they were at the back of their little field, parked between the sun and the shade, stretched out in the grass and flowers.

Ozzie followed his mama down the hill, with Ragano and Agnes trotting alongside. Kathleen sat at the picnic table and leaned down towards Ozzie.

"It's hard to imagine you could ever grow as big as those girls," she said. "But I suppose that's the way it is with pigs."

She reached down and lifted him up over her head; it wasn't easy.

"Whee piggy piggy piggy!" She sang over and over while Ozzie wiggled and giggled. "Who's my best little piggy boy?"

She sat him back on the ground and said, "It's a good thing your mama is big and strong!"

Agnes put her paws up on Kathleen's leg.

"Do you want to fly, too?" she asked. "Here goes!"

Kathleen lifted Agnes up high and sang, "Wheeee puppy puppy puppy!"

Agnes howled at the sky.

"Such a good puppy," Kathleen said, and kissed her on the nose as she put her down.

She pulled her cell phone out of her pocket and checked the time. "OK, kids, I'm on deadline. Gotta get to work. Ragano, can you watch these two out here while I do some phone interviews?"

Ragano stood at attention.

"OK," Kathleen said. "I'll be done soon!" and went into the house.

Ozzie walked away from the dogs and stared through the fence.

"Come on Ozzie!" Agnes said. "Race you around the tree!"

Ozzie said nothing.

"Come on!" Agnes said again. "What's the matter?"

Ozzie always wanted to play, but he was upset. He turned to Agnes.

"That's my game with Mama," he said.

"Huh?" Agnes replied.

"That's my game!!! My game! The piggy piggy game! Only she said puppy puppy for you. It's mine!"

"Gee, Ozzie," Agnes said. "I didn't do it on purpose. Mama just picked me up!"

"And you're always going to be small enough for her," Ozzie said. "And I'm going to be way, way too big."

"But Ozzie, you're a pig," Ragano said. "And pigs grow up. Mama can't pick me up over her head, either. I'm too big."

"Then I'm not going to grow up!" Ozzie said. "I'm going to stay Mama's baby boy forever and ever and ever!"

"But Ozzie, we all grow just as big as we're supposed to!" Ragano said. "I'm a big kind of dog, and Agnes is a small kind of dog."

"Are there small kinds of pigs?" Ozzie asked.

"I don't know," Ragano said. "I've only ever met you and the ladies up the hill. I guess maybe it's possible."

"Then I am a small kind of pig!" Ozzie said.

Ragano and Agnes looked at each other. They weren't sure that was the case, but they decided not to argue with him.

Ozzie smiled. "There! I'm a little pig and you're a little dog, Agnes! Tag! You're it!"

The two of them took off racing, while Ragano kept a close eye. Up and down and around the Japanese maple they raced, until they were very tired and flopped down in the shade. Ozzie caught his breath, then looked up the hill towards the big pigs' paddock. And there they were, the two giant sisters, staring down the hill at the piglet.

Ozzie stood up, mouth open.

"Little piglet! Baby piglet!" Harriet called out. "Please come here!"

"Oh, Sister," Ice said, "do you think he could be a baby of ours?"

"Little boy!" Harriet called. "Please come say hello! We have seen no babies for ever so long."

Ozzie slowly walked up the hill until he stood before them, just on the other side of the fence. They were huge, much bigger than Locket, but with short, stout legs.

"Child," Harriet said, "what is your name?"

"Ozzie Osboar," he replied, "I'm a rock star!" but he faltered a little on his last few words.

"Sister," said Ice, "we must offer the young one advice. This is your Aunt Harriet," she said, pointing her nose at her sister, "and I am Auntie Ice."

Ozzie was silent. Ragano and Agnes had followed him up the hill and stood just behind him.

"The life of a pig is hard," said Harriet. "Tomorrow is uncertain."

"Why?" asked Ozzie.

"It is the way it is," replied Harriet.

"So learn to swim!" Ice cried. "Beware! Beware! Beware the flood!"

"The raging waters," said Harriet, "The clinging mud!"

"The men with guns, the flowing blood!" cried Ice.

"So learn to swim," whispered Ice. "Beware the flood. . ."

Ozzie slowly backed away.

"Oh, dear," Harriet said. "Was that too much information for one so young and tender?"

"Yes," Ice replied. "Definitely a little TMI for a first meeting, I believe."

Ozzie stared hard at the gigantic aunties, slowly backing away, until he finally turned and ran to the back door as fast as his little legs could take him.

Chapter Twelve

A Turn for the Worse

The three young crows popped out of the pine tree behind the little farmhouse and flew to the top of the barn.

"I got new words!" Carlita said. "She said, 'I'm on deadline. Gotta hurry up!'"

"Say it again!" Carlyle said. "I didn't catch it all."

"You have to pay attention," Carlita said. "Spying isn't just about hiding! It's about hiding and *gathering information*."

"So say it again!" Carlos said.

"You too?" Carlita sighed.

She repeated the words over and over until the boys could also say them.

"Wait 'til Polonius finds out we learned new words all by ourselves!" Carlita said. "She'll be proud of us!"

The three crows heard horseshoes clopping on pavement; someone was riding to the airport. The horse and rider were hidden behind the trees that lined the street, but moments later, they appeared at the end of the driveway.

"Oh no, not again," Carlos said. "It's Falstaff."

"We have permission to follow them if it's for spying purposes," Carlita said. "Stay in the trees, boys!"

The crows dove from the barn roof and hopped from tree to tree just behind the horse and rider, trying to be as quiet as they could. Falstaff, however, noticed them quickly and gave them a wink as he obediently walked along. As they walked around the corner at Durley's Pond, the horse tripped over a tree branch that had fallen into the road.

"Stupid horse," Bonnie said. "That's why we call you Fall Flat instead of Falstaff. Can't even step over a branch."

"Oh, oh," said Carlos. He flew up to a branch just ahead of Falstaff, but stayed hidden in the branches. "Don't do it Falstaff. Don't buck her. She's gonna beat you again."

Falstaff whispered back as he walked along, "Yes, she will," he said. "Now go home before you get into trouble."

The crows, however, did not. They followed along, hot on his trail, using all their best spy stuff to avoid being seen. They'd been given permission to leave the farm to spy for Falstaff's sake and they weren't going to miss the opportunity.

There were no trees to hide in near Billy's, so they hung back a little when the horse and rider reached the corner of Route 63. Once they'd crossed the highway the crows quickly flew ahead of them, using the double-back technique their Uncle Wilson had taught them on his last visit.

Bonnie rode Falstaff to the edge of the woods and began to canter him around the huge field. Once. Twice. Three times. The crows watched from the trees.

"Maybe he'll behave this time," Carlyle said.

"Maybe he'll be too tired to buck her off," Carlos said.

Carlita just watched.

The pair slowed to a trot along the far side of the airport, and when they passed the hidden crows they saw Bonnie was smiling and looking very confident on the big draft. Falstaff was drenched with sweat, but moving like the amazing athlete that he was. At the farthest corner, Bonnie slowed Falstaff to a walk, and just as all three crows were letting out a collective sigh of relief, the horse reared up on his hind legs, launched himself into a gallop, then stopped dead, threw a huge buck and bolted away at light speed. Bonnie had hung on valiantly, but when Falstaff skidded to a stop she'd lost a stirrup and the mighty buck was more than she could handle. She flew through the air so high that Carlita thought Falstaff had galloped halfway across the airport before Bonnie finally hit the ground.

The crows flew after the horse, who raced across the road, which was fortunately clear of cars, and through the parking lot of the ice cream store before slowing down to a trot on Munson Road.

"Holy cats, Falstaff!" Carlos yelled when they'd caught up with him. "If you weren't going to get into so much trouble for that, I'd say that was the best thing I've ever seen!!!"

"Brilliant!" Carlyle shouted. "You ran away so fast you didn't get to see how high you tossed her!"

Carlita had hung back for a few seconds to see if Bonnie got up. She had, and she was hobbling slowly across the field.

"She's up and walking," Carlita said. "She looks real mad."

Falstaff didn't say a word. He lifted his chin a little higher as he steadily trotted down the road toward home, and the young crows followed from above.

"I am a little pig," Ozzie said. "I am a little pig. I am a *little pig*! My mama will always be able to pick me up and snuggle me and hold me high in the air and . . . wheee! And . . . I am a little pig!"

Ragano, Agnes and Ozzie were alone in the kitchen. Kathleen had gone to her office, and Ozzie was huddled under his fleece blanket in his crate. His mama always closed him in it when she left in case he accidentally walked on the tile and his legs slid out from under him. Sometimes he couldn't stand himself up again.

"Ozzie, why does it matter?" Ragano asked. "When I was a puppy Mama carried me zipped inside her jacket all the time. And then I got too big, so now I just stay next to her. We all grow up!"

"Agnes is staying small," Ozzie said. "I'm way bigger than her now!"

"I'm sorry, Ozzie," Agnes said. "I can't do anything about it. But sometimes I'd like to be bigger! I'm way too small to jump over the fence and visit in the barn the way Ragano can."

"There are good things and bad things to being every size," Ragano said. "But we are all fine the way we are."

"You saw them! You saw the auntie pigs!" Ozzie said. "They're gigantic! What if I get that big? Mama won't love me anymore. She won't snuggle me . . ."

"I've been here a few years, and I've never known Mama to stop loving anyone because they got too big," Ragano said.

"And Aggie," Ozzie said, "what were they talking about? It didn't make any sense. She said a pig's life is uncertain. Why? Because pigs grow too big and nobody loves us anymore? And why do I have to learn to swim?"

"Honestly, Ozzie," Agnes said. "Don't you think you're being a little silly?"

But Ozzie didn't think he was silly at all. Nothing meant more to him than his mama, and she loved her perfect *little* boy and he loved her. He crawled all the way under his fleece blanket and burst into tears.

Falstaff stood in his stall, waiting. The sweat dripped down his chest and shoulders, but he knew he wasn't getting a bath that day. He might not even get water until he was turned out in his paddock later, so he'd stopped in several other stalls and drank down their water buckets before he got to his own. Then he drank all the water in his, as well, since he assumed she'd hit him with it, and an empty bucket was less awful than a full one.

The crows lined up on top of his door.

"Falstaff, you gotta stop it," Carlyle said. "She's just gonna keep beating you! Let her win!"

"Yeah, Fally," Carlos said. "She's too mean. You can't win!"

"She will never break me," Falstaff said quietly. "Never."

"I dunno," Carlyle said. "If she keeps trying as hard as she is, she just might!"

"Trust me," Falstaff said, "I got this."

It was another ten minutes before Bonnie hobbled into the barn. The crows flew up into the haymow where they could stay hidden and spy.

"You nasty, rotten, stupid, fat, lazy, ugly piece of turd," Bonnie said. "I will teach you a lesson you will never forget!"

Carlita was frightened, but she'd been practicing her human talk every day and it turned out she had a gift for memorizing every word. She tried hard to focus on learning these new words and not on the terrible things that were about to happen to her friend.

Bonnie reached for the water bucket and unhooked it from the wall.

"YOU WILL LEARN!" she shouted at him, "Or I will find a way to ship you to a slaughter yard and turn you into dog food!"

And she slammed the bucket into his left front leg. Falstaff stood firm. She slammed it into his belly. Falstaff didn't flinch.

"I WILL BREAK YOU!" Bonnie shouted, and she took the bucket and slammed it into his left front leg with everything she had, and that, it seemed, was when she finally broke Falstaff, because his leg collapsed beneath him and he hobbled backwards on his three other legs.

"Knock it off," Bonnie said. "You're not hurt."

But she looked nervous. She dropped the bucket and stepped towards the horse, and he hobbled backwards into the corner. She reached down to touch him where she had hit him, and he flinched and scrunched farther away from her.

"Stand still," she said. "Let me see it."

Falstaff couldn't move any further back, so she felt his leg from top to bottom.

"Oh, wow," Bonnie muttered under her breath. "If anything's wrong with this horse Kathleen is going to fire me."

Bonnie removed Falstaff's tack and hung it on a saddle rack outside his door. She dropped his soaked saddle pad on the floor in the aisle and got his halter.

"Come on," she said. "I have to clean you up and take a look at that."

Bonnie led Falstaff into the aisle, but every time he tried to put weight on his left front foot it collapsed beneath him and Bonnie had to hold him up. It took forever to get the limping horse to the wash stall to hose him down, and the one short step up into it seemed insurmountable.

"Come on, you stupid cow!" Bonnie yelled at him. "You aren't worth the fifty cents a pound for your meat!"

For the crows watching from above, it was unbearable; all of them had tears in their eyes. When Falstaff was finally tied in the wash stall, they leaned over the ledge and the horse glanced up, gave them a small smile out of the corner of his mouth, and winked.

"Huh?" Carlos whispered. "What's that supposed to mean?"

"I think," Carlita whispered back, "it means he has a plan. . ."

By the time Kathleen got home from work the sun was low in the sky. David was in the barn setting grain buckets for the morning feeding, so Kathleen let Ozzie out of his crate and sent him into the back yard with the dogs while she made up his bottle. He was eating a lot of solid food already, but she enjoyed their feeding time together so she wasn't in a hurry to wean him from his milk replacer. She'd just finished filling his bottle when she heard a knock at the back door.

"Come on in!" she called without looking, because that's how it works with a farm kitchen; it doesn't matter who it is, they are welcome to walk through the door.

Moments later, Bonnie was in the kitchen.

"Oh, hi Bonnie," Kathleen said. "I'm really busy. What's up?"

"Well, I took Falstaff for a ride today, and he tripped over a branch in the road," she said. "I think he may have twisted something in his left front leg. He's a little lame."

"Did you give him a bute?" Kathleen asked. Bute is a medicine for horses that works like aspirin for people.

"Yes, but he's still limping," Bonnie said.

"That's odd," Kathleen said. "He's never lame."

"I know, right?" Bonnie said.

"I'll take a look at it in the morning," Kathleen said. "If he's still limping we'll have to call the vet."

"Oh, I don't think we have to do that!" Bonnie said.

"If he's lame, why wouldn't we?" Kathleen asked.

"I'm sure it's just a matter of running cold water on it a few times a day and giving him bute," Bonnie said. "It was just a little trip. He'll be fine."

"I think I'll be the judge of that," Kathleen said. "I'd rather be safe than sorry."

"Yes, of course," Bonnie said.

"I have to feed my Osboar," Kathleen said. "I'll see you in the morning."

Ragano and Agnes were romping in the back yard, but Ozzie hovered near the back door. He didn't want to be anywhere near the strange big aunties with their queer way of talking. He didn't even want to be near his best friend, little Agnes, who would always be small enough to sit on Mama's lap. Ozzie had gone from being the most happy-go-lucky little pig in the entire world to a sad little pig who carried the weight of the entire world on his shoulders. It simply wasn't fair. Why couldn't he be a small dog?

Agnes came racing down the hill.

"Come on, Ozzie!" she said. "Let's go play!"

"I don't want to," Ozzie said.

"Come on!" she said again. "We've been inside for hours! Don't you want to run?"

"I don't want to do anything," Ozzie said.

"But I do!" Agnes said, not understanding why he was sad. "Come on! Tag! You're it!"

"Stop it!" shouted Ozzie, who was now more angry than sad. "Stop it! Stop it! Stop it!"

Kathleen stepped through the back door with Ozzie's bottle, just in time to find him squealing at the top of his lungs as he lunged at Agnes and bit her on the shoulder.

Chapter Thirteen

Sink or Swim

"What do we do?" Carlos said. "Someone's got to make Bonnie stop!"

"But who?" asked Carlyle.

"I know who," said Carlita. "Come on. We have to go find Grandmother!"

The three of them took off towards the little barn where Carla could often be found hobnobbing with the old ponies in their paddock. When they arrived, however, they heard a big commotion behind the little farmhouse. Ragano was barking, Agnes was wailing, and Kathleen was yelling at the top of her lungs.

"Ozzie!" she shouted. "Don't you ever, ever, ever hurt your friend! What were you thinking?"

The crows flew over to the big pine tree and perched in the branches above the scene.

Kathleen was holding Agnes, trying to calm her down while also trying to get a look at her shoulder, where there was a splotch of bright blood against her white hair.

"Hold still, Aggie," she said. "I have to see if you need stitches."

Kathleen held her close, but she couldn't get her calm. Ozzie nuzzled at her leg, trying to get her attention.

"No Ozzie!" she shouted. "Go away! Can't you see she's bleeding?"

Ozzie had never been shouted at in his entire short life. He slowly backed away, then turned and raced to the back of the yard, sobbing. When he reached the top of the hill the auntie pigs were waiting for him at their gate.

"Oh, dear," said Harriet. "Do you see what we have here, Auntie Ice?"

"Yes, I do," Ice replied. "We have a naughty little piggy, Sister."

"And a pig's life it so uncertain, little boy," said Harriet. "Didn't we tell you to beware?"

"Beware! Beware!"

"Beware what?" Ozzie asked.

"For pigs, the future is always grim," Harriet said.

"Ozzie Osboar, learn to swim!" Ice said.

"But why?" Ozzie asked.

"Well, you will find out soon enough at the rate you're going," Harriet said. "Dear Sister, do we have anything we can offer him to eat as he was so kind to come visit us?"

"Ozzie Osboar!" Kathleen called from the back door. "You get down here right now!"

"Mama's calling me," Ozzie said, and he turned and ran back to the house.

The crows peered down from the tree as the back door slammed shut.

"We have to find Grandmother and tell her what's happening," Carlita said, "but I don't know where to start!"

Kathleen felt Falstaff's lame leg from top to bottom.

"I dunno," she said. "He's got swollen spots way up high, like welts, but that certainly wouldn't have come from a branch in the road."

"That's the only thing I know of that happened," Bonnie said. "I think he'll be fine."

"He's three-legged!" Kathleen said. "Call the vet and get her out here today!"

"I don't think he's . . ."

"Call the vet!"

It was early the next day, and Kathleen was in no mood to deal with anyone or anything. The night before had been stressful enough. Agnes hadn't needed stitches, so Kathleen cleaned out the bite and let her snuggle on her lap for the rest of the evening. Poor Aggie was now terrified of Ozzie, who had always been her best friend, and Kathleen didn't know what to do. She decided she had to put them out in separate yards. The dogs could go out in the big back yard, and Ozzie would have to stay by himself in the side yard with Percival and the ducks. She didn't know if he'd attack Agnes again, but she couldn't take a chance and leave them unsupervised.

For the first time in his life, Ozzie looked sad, and it broke her heart. That night, she'd sent him into his crate to go to sleep, and she placed his favorite red plaid fleece over him.

"Osboar, my angel, what on earth is going on with you?" she said. "You've always been such a perfect little boy, and now I don't know what to think."

"He'll be OK," David said, looking over her shoulder at the sad little pig. "It had to have been a fluke. He's never been mean to anyone."

"I love him so much," Kathleen said, "but I love Aggie, too, and I can't let him hurt her. He's so much bigger than her now. There has to be a reason."

"I guess we'll see," David said.

Kathleen closed the crate and turned out the light.

As she walked away, Ozzie thought, of course there's a reason. Mama just said it. I'm not her "perfect *little* boy" anymore. As he cried himself to sleep, it sounded exactly like he was saying, "Mama, Mama, Mama," over and over again.

The young crows didn't catch up with their grandmother until the next morning. Carla had been visiting with friends near Clover Nook Farm on the other side of town and they were having a lovely time picking through the fields for overlooked ears of corn. She hadn't arrived back on Locket's Meadow until after dark.

Carla was the smartest crow, and actually, the smartest *anybody* the young crows had ever met. She always knew how to fix every problem. It took a long time for the siblings to tell her their story, with the three of them talking over each other, but eventually Carla understood that Bonnie was a horrible person and she was hurting Falstaff. Badly.

"Oh dear," Carla said. "This is terrible. Someone certainly must do something about this."

"And now Falstaff is hurt and she did it to him!" Carlita said.

"Maybe we should go talk to him," Carla said. "Let's go."

The four of them flew into the barn, but when they saw Bonnie in the stall with him they flew right through and out the other side, then in through the open haymow door. The settled on the hay bales above the horse's stall to spy.

Bonnie was rubbing a very smelly liniment on Falstaff's leg.

"Everyone is so worried about you, but no one cares that you try to kill *me* all the time," she said. "If I get fired because of this, believe me, you will pay."

Carla noticed how roughly she rubbed the medicine on the injured horse.

"I'm not calling the vet just so she can figure out what happened and then blame me," Bonnie said. "If she wants you looked at, she can call her all by herself."

"There," she said, exiting the stall. "That should take the swelling down. You can stay inside today. Stupid horse. Since you make my life miserable, I'll make yours worse."

Falstaff had been holding his foot off the ground the entire time Bonnie was in the stall with him, but as soon as she'd left the barn, he set it flat on the floor and began to munch on his hay.

"Hmmmm," Carla said. "I think Falstaff may have figured this out by himself, but let's go see."

The four of them exited the haymow and swooped down into the barn, landing across the top of the big horse's stall.

"Hello Falstaff," Carla said. "I hear you've been having some trouble with the trainer."

Falstaff smiled. "She would tell you that she's the one having trouble with me," he said.

"It seems to me you know what you're doing," Carla said. "Do you want to talk about it?"

"Nope," Falstaff replied. "I think the fewer that know about it, the better."

"I agree," Carla said. "But you let me know if there's anything we can do to help. You hear?"

"I will, Carla," he said. "Thank you."

"Come on, children," Carla said. "We have other things to take care of."

The children obediently followed, but as soon as they settled in the tall tree behind the big barn, they broke out in a loud clatter, all three of them talking at once.

"Now, now, now," Carla said as they pelted her with questions. "You're going to have to trust me. And Falstaff. We will keep an eye out to make sure he's OK, however. So you can keep doing your spying, but please be careful and don't take any chances! That Bonnie's a crazy one!"

"Grandma," Carlita said. "There's one more thing. We didn't tell you something kinda important."

"And what is that?"

"We . . . um . . . it's a secret," Carlita said, "but the boys and I are learning how to human speak."

It was noon time when Kathleen finished her phone interviews, so she decided to take a short break before she wrote her stories for the day. She picked up her phone and dialed Bonnie.

"Hello?" Bonnie answered.

"Hi, Bonnie," Kathleen replied. "What did the vet say about Falstaff?"

"Oh, I didn't call yet."

"What?!"

"I didn't call yet."

"I heard that part," Kathleen said. "What I'm asking is, why not!?"

"I just didn't," Bonnie said.

"Call now!" Kathleen said.

"As soon as I'm done teaching this lesson," Bonnie said.

"Call and then let me know when she's coming," Kathleen said. "This is your job!"

"Yes," Bonnie said.

Kathleen hung up the phone. She decided to write one quick article and then go to the barn and talk to the belligerent Bonnie. What was the point, she wondered, of having a barn manager if she couldn't get her to do her job? Ozzie was napping in his crate and the dogs were loose in the kitchen, but it was a nice, cool fall day so Kathleen decided to send them outside for a while. She sent the dogs into the back yard through the back kitchen door, watching Agnes as she limped slightly on her sore leg. She sighed, then opened Ozzie's crate and woke him up.

"Come on, Osboar," she said. "Time to go outside for a little while. The weather's too nice to stay inside."

Ozzie didn't move, but Kathleen reached in and gave him a big nudge.

"Come on, little boy, you need to get exercise," she said.

The piglet shuffled out of the crate and stood looking up at his mama.

"Let's go! Outside!"

She gave his butt a push in the direction of the mudroom door to go out into the ducks' yard.

"No, no Mama!" Ozzie said.

"What?" She gave him another push.

"No, no, no, no Mama!" Ozzie said as she pushed him along the hallway.

"I must be hearing things," Kathleen mumbled. "Let's go, Osboar!"

"No, no, no, no!" Ozzie squealed. "Mama, Mama, Mama!"

"I'm losing my mind," Kathleen said. "You can't be talking!"

She opened the door and followed him outside. He stood on the sidewalk and looked up at her. Kathleen knelt down and stroked his back. He was almost as tall as her knees, now, and growing so fast. She was going to miss him being a lap pig, but those days were just about over.

"My handsome little boy," she said. "You be good. I have just one quick article to write, and then I'll let you guys back in."

The dogs were sniffing around in the wildflowers. All would be fine for the next fifteen minutes, she thought, so she went to her office and sat at her desk that looked over the duck yard where Ozzie was.

Ozzie stood at the back door and looked up the hill at Agnes and Ragano playing in the wildflowers. He wandered over to where Percival and the lady ducks were sleeping alongside the pond. Maybe they would talk to him.

"Hello," Ozzie said.

Percival untucked her head from beneath her wing.

"Hello," she replied. "What are you doing here all alone?"

"I'm in trouble," Ozzie said. "I bit Agnes."

Percival stood up.

"You aren't going to bite anyone else, are you?" she asked.

"I don't think so," Ozzie replied. "I was just angry. I'm not angry anymore. I'm just sad."

"I am sorry you are sad," Percival said. "You always seem like such a happy little fellow."

"I was," Ozzie said. "But not anymore."

"Hmmm," said the wise old goose. "Why is that, do you think?"

"What if my mama doesn't love me when I'm big?"

"Hmmmm," Percival said. "You know your mama's daughter, Bo, don't you?"

"Yes," Ozzie answered.

"Do you think she loves her?" Percival asked.

"Of course she does!" Ozzie answered, confused. "Mama calls her 'baby girl!'"

"Do you know that Bo was once much smaller than you and Kathleen could pick her up and snuggle her on her lap, and then she grew?"

Ozzie was quiet for a moment.

"Ragano said Mama used to carry him inside her jacket everywhere she went," Ozzie said. "She used to carry me in a little pink bag, but I don't fit in it anymore."

"And Mama stopped loving Ragano when he didn't fit in her jacket anymore?"

"Of course not!" Ozzie said. "Of course she loves Ragano!"

"Hmmmm," Percival said.

"I think I need to think," Ozzie said.

"I think you do as well!" Percival said, waddling to the edge of the little pond to take a drink.

The pond was a small one that they had built just for ducks when they first bought the little farmhouse. It had a small deep pool on top with a waterfall that dropped to a slightly bigger pool and another waterfall to an even bigger pool. There was a pump that sent the water round and round and round so there was always water flowing over the waterfalls.

"Hey Percival," Ozzie asked. "How hard is it to swim?"

"Not hard at all," Percival said. "You just go into the water, and you swim."

Kathleen had finished her article. She'd thought about walking next door to see what time the vet was coming, but decided to call Bonnie, instead.

"Hello," Bonnie said.

"Hi," Kathleen replied. "What time is the vet coming?"

"Oh, I didn't call yet."

"You're kidding me."

"No," Bonnie replied.

"Never mind," Kathleen said, and hung up the phone.

She dialed the vet's office. It was already afternoon and she knew there was little chance of getting an appointment for that day, but she had to try. It turned out that Dr. Stacey was in the area that afternoon and could check on Falstaff after her last stop of the day, and Kathleen thanked her, hung up the phone and flopped down into her office chair. She wasn't sure what to do about Bonnie, but clearly she had to do something.

She dialed her daughter.

"Hey, Mama," Bo said.

"Help," Kathleen said. "Why do I have so much trouble finding decent help for the farm?"

"What happened now?" Bo asked.

Kathleen quickly told the story of the belligerent Bonnie.

"That's an easy one," Bo said. "Fire her."

"How can I?" Kathleen asked. "I don't have time to organize all the barn stuff and teach lessons and call the vet and . . ."

"You asked," Bo said. "That's the only solution I have. There comes a point where you have to organize your priorities, and the horses are a priority."

"I don't think I'm ready yet," Kathleen said. "I have to go check on Ozzie. I'll talk to you later."

She hung up and looked out the window to see what Ozzie was doing. At first she didn't see him, but then . . . what she thought was a goose taking a bath in the uppermost pond . . . was actually a little pig, thrashing about in the water, desperately trying to stay afloat.

Chapter Fourteen

The Promise

"What do you mean you're learning to speak human?" Carla asked.

"I mean we're learning to speak human," Carlita said.

Carla sighed. She had thought the toughest job she'd ever have was raising Carl and his buddy Wilson, but these grandchildren were equally challenging, which is why she spent so much time these days visiting friends off the farm. Retirement from motherhood, it seemed, was not an option for her unless perhaps she flew to Florida as some of the other older crows in the neighborhood had done after a particularly hard winter.

"All right, young lady," Carla said. "I need a better explanation than that."

"It's simple," Carlita said. "Listen . . . 'No, no mama!'" The "no, no Mama" came out human, loud and clear.

Carla gasped.

"And you boys?" she asked. "You can do this, as well?"

The boys were silent. They were afraid to get into trouble with Carla.

"Oh, just do it!" Carlita snapped.

Carlos finally gave in. "You nasty, rotten, stupid, fat, lazy, ugly piece of turd," he said.

And Carlyle chimed in, "I will teach you a lesson you will never forget!"

Carla's beak dropped open. "Where did you ever hear something like that?" she asked.

"Bonnie said it to Falstaff," Carlos said. "Me and Carlyle weren't paying attention, but Carlita got it all and taught it to us."

Carla wanted to ask Carlita if she was sure she got the words correct, but if there was one thing she knew about her granddaughter, as spunky as she could be, she was incredibly smart and she never lied. Carla had heard about crows that could talk, but only those kept in cages in zoos, like the cage birds in the little farmhouse. She had a friend who used to visit the Beardsley Park Zoo in Bridgeport and who had told her the caged crow there could say, "Coca Cola" and a few other small words, but entire sentences of human? It didn't seem possible.

"How did this start?" Carla asked.

"Ozzie Osboar was practicing saying 'Mama' in human talk," Carlita answered, "and we tried it, too. And then we learned how to say 'no, no.' And Falstaff, Captain and James told us if we wanted to help get rid of Bonnie, we needed to learn more words, so we talked to Polonius, the cage bird, and she taught us more," Carlita paused. "Is it bad, Grandmother?"

"No," Carla replied. "It's just different. Can you do me a favor? Can you keep this very, very secret? I think the horses are right and you may be able to help Falstaff, but it has to be a surprise. Don't let any of the humans hear you. Do you understand?"

"Yes, Grandmother," the three crows responded.

"And don't tell your father about any of this, either," Carla said. "The last thing I need is for him to get involved. I've already spent way too much of my time cleaning up the messes he made when he was your age."

"Ozzie!!" Kathleen yelled and ran through the laundry room and out the side door. "Ozzie!!!"

She raced to the top of the pond, which was quite deep and had straight, slippery walls with no place for a pig to grab onto with a smooth hoof to climb his way out. Ozzie was frantically paddling, nose above water, gasping for breath. Kathleen dropped to her knees and grabbed him around the belly and hauled him out of the water. She picked him up and held him to her chest, soaking herself right through her clothes, but she hardly noticed. All she could think about was getting him warm and dry and making sure he wasn't hurt.

There were clean towels and blankets stacked in the mudroom, and she set a shivering Ozzie down and wrapped him first in a towel and then a fleece blanket. The air had the chill of autumn in it, and the pond water was cold from the frosty night air. Kathleen had no idea how long he'd been in the water, but he felt very cold to her touch.

She bundled her pig up like a baby and sat on the garden rock just above where Duck was buried and rocked her pig back and forth, sobbing.

"Oh, Ozzie Osboar," she cried. "What on earth am I going to do with you?"

Ragano and Agnes stood on the other side of the fence, watching.

"Captain," Kathleen said. "You have the key. I know you do. I need to be able to understand all of you. I used to be able to. What's wrong with me now?"

Kathleen had held Ozzie for an hour until she was sure he was good and warm and breathing well. He was exhausted, so she put him in his crate, covered him with a heavy fleece and rubbed his belly until he was sound asleep. She stared at him for a long while, with Ragano sitting on one side of her and Agnes on the other. It had been a terrible few days with her young pig, and she had no idea why.

Why couldn't she understand? She'd changed into dry clothes, put her work boots on and headed next door to have a conversation with the one animal she could hear clearer than all the rest. She'd grabbed Captain's halter from the barn and hiked up to his paddock and led him down to the grassy area outside the indoor arena. She sat next to him on the ground and the horse dropped his head and grazed.

"Come on Captain," she said. "Help me. Teach me. I need to understand."

Captain said nothing, but he looked at her with sympathetic eyes as he took mouthful after mouthful of grass and slowly munched on it.

The sound of the horse chewing was very soothing, and before she knew it, Kathleen was feeling calm for the first time in days. She leaned back on her elbows and closed her eyes, feeling the warmth of the afternoon sun on top of her head. She was so relaxed she began to think about how nice it would be to take a nap on the grass while Captain munched alongside her when she heard a voice say, "Mama, we are all talking to you all day long, if you would only take the time to listen."

Kathleen opened her eyes and sat up. Captain had stopped eating grass and was looking at her with soft, sad eyes. Had she really heard what she thought she had?

But, as always, there was no time to think about it. She heard the distinct sound of a diesel engine, and she looked up to see Dr. Stacey's truck bumping along the gravel as she turned into the farm driveway.

Carla flapped her way over to the little barn as quickly as she could. The ponies were standing quietly in the paddock and she landed squarely on Classy's back.

"What on earth happened over here?" Carla asked. "Is Ozzie OK?"

Locket sighed. Ragano, of course, had jumped the fence that morning and told her that Ozzie had bitten Agnes, and they had all heard the commotion when Kathleen found Ozzie in the pond.

"How did you find out?" Locket asked.

"I overheard Kathleen asking the doctor to check on Ozzie after she examines Falstaff," Carla said. "Why in heaven's name would he go in the pond?"

"Percival said the auntie pigs keep telling Ozzie he has to learn how to swim," Classy said. "And of course, a goose would say it's easy, just jump in and paddle your legs."

"Apparently he has some natural swimming ability," Cressida said, "or he would have drowned for certain."

"What is going on with that young man?" Carla sighed. "And why would those pigs say something like that to him? Who could have guessed that a little pig would cause such a ruckus on a farm?"

"If anyone had bothered to ask me," Cressida said, "I would have said so."

"Now Cressie," Calypso said, "we don't know what's going on inside his head. He's growing big so quickly, but he's really only a few months old. We may be expecting too much from one who is just a child."

"Here comes Kathleen," Classy said, and Carla flapped off her back and onto the barn roof.

Kathleen was talking on her cell phone as she approached on the path from the big barn.

"It's the strangest thing, Baby," she said, clearly talking to David on the phone. "Stacey did all the lameness tests and there was nothing wrong. The X-rays were perfect. But as soon as Bonnie took his lead rope to walk him he absolutely refused to put any weight on his leg."

She paused.

"Bonnie? I asked her point blank why she refused to call the vet," she said. "She told me she didn't realize that's what I meant, and I hadn't made myself clear. She apologized for misunderstanding me. Is it me? Am I crazy? How much clearer do I have to be than 'call the vet'?"

Another pause.

"I don't know," she said. "I can't think about it right now. Stacey's driving over from next door to take a look at Osboar. I'm so worried he might catch pneumonia from inhaling water. I know that's what happened to Ice in the Iowa flood. And I still have to finish two articles before five o'clock."

Kathleen walked past the horses and into the barn, then out the other side, and the eavesdroppers heard no more.

Carla swooped down past the ladies in the paddock.

"I think I need to have a conversation with the auntie pigs," she said, and flapped up the hill towards their paddock.

Ozzie was sound asleep in his crate under his fleece blanket. When he first woke up he hadn't remembered what had happened over the past few days. Then, it all came flooding back to him, and he squinted his eyes closed. He tried to fall back to sleep so he could forget it again, but all he could see was water splashing all around him, and he remembered how desperately he'd tried to paddle his legs the way the goose had told him, but the harder he tried the harder it was to stay afloat. He gave up trying to sleep and opened his eyes to find Ragano and Agnes staring at him. Ozzie moaned and closed his eyes again.

"We know you're awake," Agnes said.

Ozzie opened his eyes and rolled up onto his belly. The world had never seen such an ashamed little pig, and he didn't know what to do as he squirmed beneath their gazes.

"Are you OK?" Agnes asked.

"I think so," Ozzie mumbled. "Are you OK?"

"I think so," Agnes said.

Ragano walked to the other side of the kitchen and left them alone.

"Some rock star, huh?" Ozzie said.

"Why did you bite me?" Agnes asked. "We were best friends."

"I don't know," Ozzie said. "I was just so . . . mad. You didn't do anything. It was just me."

Ozzie paused to think about what Agnes had just said. "Wait," he said. "Does that mean we aren't friends anymore?"

His eyes filled with tears.

"I can't be friends with someone who will bite me," Agnes said. "I can't be best friends with someone I can't trust."

"But I won't ever do that again!" Ozzie cried. "I won't ever hurt you!"

"How do I believe you?" Agnes asked.

"I promise!" Ozzie said. "I promise I will never, ever be a bad pig again!"

"Just one more chance," Agnes said. "That's it."

"I can do it," Ozzie said. "I promise and promise and promise. I will always be a good pig forever and ever."

"And you will never go in the pond again?" Ragano asked from the kitchen door where he had planted his front feet against the window to watch for his mama.

"You don't have to worry about that," Ozzie said.

"Well there," Ragano said. "That's all done. Mama is just getting back, and the doctor is in the driveway."

Ragano barked so Kathleen would know he was doing his job, and Agnes raced to the door and joined him. Moments later, Kathleen and Dr. Stacey came into the kitchen.

"He's in his crate," Kathleen said. "Please check him over. I don't know how long he was in the water."

She knelt down and opened the door to the crate. Ozzie usually stood up and ran to her, but this time he didn't.

"Come on, Ozzie Bear," she said. "Are you OK?"

She reached in and lifted him to his feet and pulled him out onto the floor.

"What's the matter, angel?" she asked. "Please tell me you're OK."

Dr. Stacey squatted down next to him and put the stethoscope into her ears.

"I have to listen to his heart and his lungs," she said.

Ozzie stood perfectly still while the doctor listened carefully for a long time. She finally stopped and shrugged.

"I don't hear anything," she said. "I'm guessing he's fine, but we may want to put him on antibiotics just to be safe."

"So you just examined two of my animals, but nothing is wrong with either of them," Kathleen said, sitting on a kitchen chair. "Yet my horse is limping, and my pig looks miserable. Can someone please remind me why I wanted to have a farm in the first place? On days like today it's hard to remember."

Ragano walked over to his mama and licked her hand.

"I know, puppy dog," Kathleen said, reaching down to rub his ears. "Thank you. I remember now."

Ozzie walked over to his mama to nudge her with his snout, but he stepped off the carpet and his legs slid out from beneath him. Kathleen reached down and lifted him onto her lap. He didn't really fit anymore, but neither of them minded.

"He's still slipping on his back legs?" Stacey asked.

"Only when he's on the kitchen tile or a really smooth surface," Kathleen answered. "Otherwise he's fine."

"Stand him up," Stacey said.

She felt the muscles in his back legs from top to bottom.

"Hmmm," she said. "His legs are still very weak. You know runts are runts for a reason, and there may be a congenital deformity in his hind end. It can't be good for him to keep slipping on the floor like that." She sighed, then added, "He may never have very strong hind legs," she added, "and as he gets heavier it'll be harder for him to support himself. Either you have to carpet the whole kitchen or he needs to be outside where the traction is better."

"Osboar outside?" Kathleen said. "I never really thought about that."

"You do know that most pigs live outside, don't you?" Stacey asked.

"But he's not like most pigs," Kathleen said. "At least I don't think so."

"Unless you can keep him from slipping," Stacey said, "this pig needs to be on better footing, and that means outside."

And that is the exact moment when Ozzie's week went from really bad to much worse.

Carla landed on the roof of Harriet and Ice's shed. The sisters were snuggled inside beneath a perfectly groomed mound of fresh straw, and Ice was snoring. Carla hopped to the ground and peered inside.

"Excuse me ladies," Carla said. "I'm sorry to bother you, but may I have a few minutes of your time?"

Harriet opened one eye.

"Sister," she said, "there is a black bird here to see us. I believe it is of the variety they call 'crow.'"

Ice awoke mid-snore and made a noise like a lawn mower sputtering. She lifted her head and gave it a great shake that sent bits of straw flying out of her giant ears, then inspected Carla with her blue eye.

"Why Sister," she said, "I do believe it *is* a crow! We had them in Iowa, as well. Of course, I never saw them until we had to swim. I only heard them calling through the windows."

"Hello, ladies," Carla said. "We haven't formally met, but my name is Carla."

"Delighted," said Harriet.

"Charmed, I am sure," said Ice. "We haven't made the acquaintance of very many of the other residents at this facility, but of course, that is by choice."

"Yes," said Harriet. "We mustn't get attached to anyone. It might inhibit us when we have to escape."

"Escape?" asked Carla. "Why would you want to escape from Locket's Meadow? Aren't you happy here?"

"Of course we are! We have found pig nirvana!" Harriet said. "The bedding is clean, we can run through the grass and wildflowers. We stretch our legs whenever we like!"

"We can lie in the sun or the shade or the mud," Ice said. "And there are bananas in the food buckets!"

"So why would you want to leave?" Carla asked.

"My dear," Harriet said, "the flood waters may rise!"

"Or the men with guns may arrive," Ice said.

"Or worst of all," Harriet said, and both pigs finished the sentence together, "the cages may come."

"We will never go back into another cage," Ice said.

"We have already turned that page," Harriet added. "We would unleash our rage!"

"And then make a mighty fast run for it," Ice said.

"Do you understand there are no cages like that here?" Carla asked.

"Maybe not now," Harriet said, "but who knows when that will change? Life cannot be trusted."

"We spent years in the cages, only to be freed by the flood," Ice said. "We told the boy pig he must learn to swim!"

"Yes, he must learn to swim!" Harriet said.

"Wow," Carla said. "Those cages really did a job on you. Make yourselves comfortable, and I'll tell you a story about where you live now and why you don't have to worry about cages or floods. Let's start with floods. Ladies, you live on top of a very big hill . . ."

Within twenty minutes the auntie pigs had a very different perspective on life.

"My goodness," Harriet said. "So you're saying we will stay at this place always?"

"And there will be no floods?" Ice asked.

"As long as water continues to run downhill, that's my guess," Carla said.

The ladies had looked at each other, both a little excited and a little confused.

"So that means the boy pig is also staying?" Harriet asked.

"Of course he is," Carla replied. "Kathleen loves him."

"We've never seen a baby stay," Harriet said.

"Babies are always snatched away," said Ice, with a hint of sadness in her voice.

"This is a game changer, Sister," Harriet said. "We could . . . make friends."

"Everyone here is quite friendly," Carla said.

Ice walked out of their shed and looked down the length of their long paddock, all the way to the back, where they loved to lie in the sun. Then she turned and looked through the gate at the yard filled with grass and flowers.

"Then this is ours?" she'd said, eyes filling with tears. "Do you think," she asked, "maybe Kathleen could love us, too?"

"I'm pretty sure she already does," Carla replied.

Chapter Fifteen

A Slippery Situation

Ozzie lifted his head and peeked out from beneath his blanket. The mudroom had windows on three sides, so when the sun began to rise behind him, he could see the quiet, pink glow reflected in the soft clouds of the western sky. He'd gotten to know what time of day it was based on where the sun was in the sky, and he knew it would only be a few more minutes before Mama came outside with his bowl of warm mash. Moments later David would follow and head to the barns to start feeding the other animals.

The mudroom wasn't the worst place for a young pig. The door to the side yard was always open so he could go in and out whenever he wanted. He couldn't go near the pond anymore because his mama had built a new fence the day after he'd gone swimming. It was sometimes lonely. Mama spent as much time as she could out in the yard with him, often bringing her laptop outside to do her work.

She also brought Ragano and Agnes out with her, but she was afraid to leave them alone with Ozzie. He seemed fine, but she was still worried he might bite someone again. She couldn't possible know that Ozzie had vowed to be the best behaved little pig in the entire world.

Every evening, Mama came out to the mudroom and turned on the heat lamp. Ozzie trotted inside and flopped down on his soft bed beneath it, and Mama covered him with a fluffy fleece blanket, nice and warm from the clothes dryer. Then she would tell him stories and sing songs, rubbing his belly until he fell asleep. It wasn't like the kitchen where he had the company of the dogs all the time, but he could lie in the sun whenever he wanted during the day, and sometimes interesting things happened in the yard.

Weeks had passed and Ozzie was nearly twice as big as he'd been when he'd gone into the pond. Kathleen could barely lift him off the ground, and certainly couldn't get him over her head. Now that he wasn't on the slippery tile, Kathleen could leave him outside and not close him in a crate when she was gone. Usually he napped under his blankets in the corner of the mudroom where the sun shined through the windows and kept him toasty warm. Even on quiet days there was something to watch, like delivery people coming and going, and he was always happy to greet them on the sidewalk and get a scratch.

Sometimes, however, people stopped by who weren't used to Locket's Meadow. One day a deliveryman came to the back door with a package that had to be signed for. Kathleen was next door at the big barn, and Ozzie was asleep beneath his blankets in the corner of the mudroom, but when he heard the knock on the door and the dogs barking inside, he jumped to his feet and barked a greeting. The deliveryman screamed and backed away, then ran out the door, and Ozzie followed him down the sidewalk, wondering why the man was running away so quickly. He jumped over the gate and raced to his car, then sped out of the driveway. A little later he returned with Kathleen, whom he had found in the barn next door, and she introduced him to Ozzie and explained that it was OK to leave packages at the back door even with a pig on guard.

"I didn't know if he would eat the package!" The man said, still shaking. "I didn't know if he'd eat me!"

"Ozzie Osboar?" Kathleen said, laughing. "He's a good pig. Don't worry about him."

She didn't mention he had once bitten a small dog, but there was no point to that. He'd always been a very good pig with people.

Ozzie was doing his best to be the best-behaved pig in the whole world. He was polite and greeted everyone with a smile. He waited patiently for his food to be set in front of him and never knocked his dish over. He came when he was called and went to sleep when it was time. But still . . . sometimes . . . he was very, very lonely.

Kathleen sat at her desk staring at her laptop screen. She wasn't writing an article; rather, she was staring at the balance of her checking account, which was dwindling down to nothing. The veterinarian bills were overwhelming, and she didn't know what to do. It had started with Falstaff and his limp. He'd stayed inside for a few days, and when it seemed he was a little better, they turned him out in the paddock with the other boys. He was perfectly fine until Bonnie decided to take him for a ride, and as soon as she put his head in the halter, his front leg went right out from beneath him. When the vet came out to check him again, she still found nothing wrong.

Bonnie lost patience waiting for Falstaff to get better, so she asked Kathleen if she could ride Beatrice instead. Kathleen had a bad feeling about it, but had no real reason to say no. However, after one ride to the airport, Beatrice came home lame in her hind end, and when the vet came out to check her, she found nothing wrong. Then Bonnie asked to ride Star instead, and one ride later his back was so sore that he flinched whenever anyone tried to put a saddle on him. The most recent vet bill came when Bonnie tried to ride Ernie, who came home limping on a front foot. After that, Kathleen told Bonnie she didn't think it was a good idea for her to ride anyone else since they were running out of horses for the lesson program, and she was running out of money to pay for lameness exams and vet bills. It was very strange that there was no explanation for any of their problems.

The horses seemed fine while out in the paddocks, but every time they seemed well enough to be ridden, their issues flared up. Stacey wondered if they all had Lyme disease, which would make them ache. The next step would be to take their blood and have it tested for Lyme. Kathleen stared at her checking account balance and knew it wasn't possible until they'd saved up some money, and that would only happen if there weren't any other medical emergencies.

Again she wondered what she had gotten herself and her poor husband into.

The weather in October could be tricky in Bethany. The temperatures dropped very low at night, while during the day it was often quite warm in the sunlight. Daybreak sometimes brought surprises, like the first morning the grass had frost on it. Ozzie awoke with the sun, and, despite his heat lamp and soft blankets, he felt an extra chill on his nose. Instead of getting up and greeting the day he took his time waking up, and he watched the sun brighten the grass only to find it had turned white during the night. Now that was an adventure! He crawled out from beneath his blankets and went outside into a sugar-coated world, slipping a little on the step down into the yard, but catching himself quickly. He nosed at the grass and took a nibble, and found it was delicious when icy. His feet left little V-shaped prints in the grass, and he walked around in circles so he could meet the tracks he had made, then did it again. He stopped for a few minutes to eat the warm breakfast Kathleen brought out for him, then went right back to trekking around in the frosty grass. Ozzie was sad when the sun rose higher in the sky, melting the frost and ending his games.

A few days later, Ozzie again felt a chilly nip in the air and opened his eyes to see the palest reflection of light in the western sky. He wondered if there was more frost, so he decided to get up early and investigate. This time, however, every single blade of grass and every green leaf on the Japanese maple was completely coated in shiny ice! The sparkle was dazzling beneath the porch light, and Ozzie couldn't wait to get outside and play in it. He trotted right out the door, only this time, he slipped on a sheet of ice and his legs went right out from beneath him. He landed, splay-legged, on the icy sidewalk.

Ozzie had a hard time getting up from the slip, so he held still for a minute, thinking about it. Maybe, he thought, this new shiny stuff wasn't meant for playing on. Finally he decided to try to inch forward until he could get his feet on the grass. It took a few tries, but his front hooves finally reached the lawn, and he stood up, but before he could get his back end to follow, his hind end slid out from beneath him. This time, instead of splaying out, they both went in the same direction. And that's when Ozzie knew he was in real trouble because it hurt. It hurt *a whole lot.*

Chapter Sixteen

The Plot Thickens

Kathleen awoke with an uneasy feeling. There was no particular reason, really. Something just felt . . . wrong. She looked through the bedroom window where the palest light glowed softly in the eastern sky, just enough to reveal an icy coating on each branch of every tree.

"Huh," she said. "Baby, do you remember anyone predicting freezing rain for last night?"

"Nope," he said.

"Me neither," Kathleen replied. "I'd have shut the back door so Ozzie couldn't get out. He never wakes up this early, but I'm going to close him inside until we can sand the sidewalk."

She pulled on a sweatshirt, as the upstairs of the old house didn't have heat so it was quite cold, then trotted down the stairs with the dogs at her feet. She opened the back door and sent Ragano and

Agnes outside, then stopped at the kitchen sink to pour a cup of coffee. She looked out the window at the back porch and screamed.

Kathleen never screamed. She had fallen off horses and broken several ribs at a time and never said a word. She'd been squished between young, angry horses and never flinched. Captain had broken her finger, and she hadn't made a sound. She'd stepped on nails that went through her feet, broken her elbow in a dog-walking accident, and shut her own hand in the truck door and never made more than a slight grunt. She'd had toes crushed by giant draft horses and never stopped working until much later in the day, when she could barely get her foot out of her boot because it was so swollen, but she never uttered a word.

So when Kathleen screamed, her husband raced down the stairs to see what had happened.

"Where are you?" he shouted when he reached the kitchen. "What's the matter?"

"It's Ozzie!" he heard her yell from the yard. "Help!!"

David ran out to the mudroom and found Kathleen on her knees just outside the door trying to lift her pig to his feet, but she was also slipping on the ice so it wasn't easy.

"Hang on!" David said, and he joined her on the sidewalk.

With one on either side of him, they lifted Ozzie and slowly got him back into the mudroom and shut the door.

Kathleen collapsed on the floor next to him.

"Ozzie Bear," she said. "What are you doing up so early? Are you OK? My poor little baby!"

She was so upset to see him trapped on the ice, flailing to get up.

Ozzie stood very still. It hurt his back to move. He'd only been on the ground for a few minutes, but it seemed like a longer stretch of time than his entire life had been up to that point. What had begun as a burning sensation in his spine had become a sharp pain that ran from his back right down his hind legs. It hurt so badly his ears were ringing, but he heard his mama tell him he needed to go to his blankets and lie down. He slowly walked to his corner, but his back legs no longer bent at the knees, so he slowly, slowly shuffled, stiff-legged, until he got to his blankets. Instead of turning around so he could see out the door, as he always did, he inched his way onto his belly facing the wall, landing with a loud groan.

"Baby, there's something really wrong with him," Ozzie heard Mama say through the ringing in his ears. "I'm calling the vet."

The sun was up, and the horses were waiting in their paddocks for their morning hay. It was taking extra long for Bonnie to feed, since the driveway was still icy, but the paddocks had rougher footing so the horses could walk safely. Bonnie got to Falstaff's paddock and stood staring at him.

"I don't think there's anything wrong with you," she said. "I watch you out here. I see you moving around just fine. As soon as I come near you with a halter you fall apart. You are a waste of space. So I'm going to get you out of here, send you someplace for rehab, and then sneak you out of there and off to the auction. I know how to do it. Everyone will think you were stolen! I can get you sold and on a trailer to a feedlot so fast nobody will know what happened. Just you wait, you miserable, lazy animal."

Bonnie aimed the flakes of hay right at Falstaff's face.

"I have never let a horse get away with your kind of garbage before," she said, "and I'm certainly not about to now."

She walked down the hill, leaving the boys to stare after her.

Moments later the three young crows fluttered down out of the birch tree that grew alongside the paddock. They landed on the fence in front of Falstaff, Captain, and James.

"That's it," Carlita said. "Now we really, really, really need a plan. She's crazy!"

"We gotta find a way to make the humans to get rid of her," Carlyle said.

"This farm isn't safe for anybody with her here!" Carlos said.

"Mama won't send Falstaff away," Captain said. "She's bluffing."

"What if she isn't?" Carlita said.

"Come on," Carlos said. "Let's follow her."

"Time to spy!" Carlyle said, and the three of them flew down to the barn where Bonnie had slipped into her shiny new pickup truck, which was parked beneath the spindly pine tree that grew next to the side door of the barn. She'd left her truck door open, and she sat with her feet dangling out the side, shoulders hunched over her cell phone. The crows perched in the pine boughs above.

"I spoke with the director at the equine rehab center, and they'll have an opening early next week," Bonnie said. "It's really absurd to keep a horse on the farm that can't do any work. Why not try to get him sound again?"

"Oh no," she said after a pause. "I'm sorry. I didn't realize your pig was injured. I understand you're upset. We can talk about this later. But if we don't act pretty quickly that spot will fill and we won't be able to get Falstaff fixed up. He's such a talented horse it would be a terrible shame."

The crows could hear Kathleen's voice get louder at the other end of the phone.

"OK," Bonnie said. "I'm sorry. You're right. Now isn't the time. Let me know how Ozzie is later. I'll cross my fingers it's nothing major. Give him a kiss on the nose for me!"

She hung up the phone. "As if I care about a stupid pig," she said.

She swung her legs inside her truck, slammed the door closed, and started the engine. The three crows raced off to find their grandmother.

"How do you do?" Harriet said. "I am Harriet and this is my sister, Ice. We've decided to make a fresh start. We haven't been very sociable since we arrived."

The two sows had approached the north side of their paddock near the horses' fence and stood there until Classy noticed them and walked over to investigate. It was the first time since their first night in the barn that the sisters had acknowledged her, preferring to stay in their shed or walk to the very back of their paddock to take naps.

"And I am Classy," the Arab said.

"I remember," Ice said. "I'm afraid we have been very, very rude. You see, we thought we were only here temporarily, but were informed by a crow . . . yes, a crow, of all creatures! . . . that we . . . could be . . . here on a permanent basis, which means we can now make friends without worrying they are a liability."

"Friends can be a liability?" Classy asked.

"When you love them and you have to leave," Ice said, "it is very painful. So we decided we'd keep it just the two of us. Sisters take care of each other, you know."

Locket had joined them at the fence and overheard the end of the conversation.

"Friends take care of each other, too," Locket said. "At least that's what we do here." She paused, then said, "you remember me. I'm Locket."

"Yes, yes, my dear," Harriet said. "The voice in the darkness."

Calypso and Cressida arrived at the fence.

"Well," Cressida said. "Look who's being chatty!"

"Be nice, Cressie," Calypso said. "They've had a rough time."

"I apologize," Cressida said. "You're right."

The back door slammed shut, and within seconds Ragano sailed over the fence and raced to the back of the yard where the paddocks met each other.

"Ozzie's hurt!" he shouted. "Ozzie slipped on the ice and now he's hurt! The doctor's coming soon!"

Carla and her three grandchildren dove out of the sky and landed on the fence between the paddocks.

"We have a problem," Carla said, "and we need a plan right now!"

Dr. Stacey hung her stethoscope around her neck and sighed.

"Well, there's no question he's in a lot of pain," she said. "But it's almost impossible for me to figure out what's causing it without x-rays. And I don't know as much about pigs as some other vets do. I think you really need to take him to a specialist where they can x-ray his back. Meanwhile I can give him medicine to ease the pain."

"My poor sweet baby," Kathleen said. "Why does everything happen to you?"

"It's the problem with runts," Stacey said. "They seldom survive because they have things wrong with them. Ozzie has a weak hind end, and there really isn't any kind of rehabilitation that I know of for a pig. No one tries to cure an injured pig. They slaughter them and eat them."

"Well, that's never going to happen," Kathleen said. "By the way, I wanted to talk to you about something before you go. Bonnie's been trying to get me to send Falstaff out to an equine rehabilitation center. What do you think?"

"I don't know," Stacey said. "We haven't even figured out what's wrong with him to try to fix it. I guess it's up to you."

"Frankly, with all the vet bills lately, we can't afford it," Kathleen said, "even if I wanted to let him leave the farm, which I don't."

"Well, then, you have your answer," Stacey said.

"I guess so," Kathleen replied.

"Oh, and Ozzie shouldn't be walking down that step to go outside," Stacey added. "You need to move him to an outside area with a shed immediately so he doesn't hurt himself even worse."

"I knew you were going to say that," Kathleen said. "I can't stand him being even further away from me."

"That's the only way you can keep him safe," Stacey said.

"Yes," Kathleen replied, blinking back tears; she had never cried over any animal as much as she had for Ozzie. "We can build a little shed right behind the house in the vegetable garden. The fencing is already there so it'll be easy."

"I'll get his medicine from the truck," Stacey said. "You need to make an appointment to bring Ozzie to Massachusetts. Take him to the Cummings School of Veterinary Medicine at Tufts University. When you call, ask for the large animal clinic. I'll write the number down for you."

"Yes," Kathleen said, gently rubbing Ozzie's shoulder.

She couldn't believe how well behaved he'd been considering everything the doctor did to him. While Stacey poked and prodded,

Kathleen had held her breath, terrified that he'd bite her the way he'd bitten Agnes. Even though he'd grunted and squealed from the pain, he was never once aggressive.

She decided to work from home that day so she could keep a close eye on him.

Dr. Stacey was rummaging around in her black bag, clearly looking for something.

"Did you see what I did with my truck keys?" she asked. "I was sure they were in my bag."

Kathleen sighed.

"Hang on," she said, "I'll go check the fridge."

Ozzie kept perfectly still, head on his front hooves. If he didn't move at all, it didn't hurt quite so much. He tried not to think of the pain. Instead, he thought about the promise he had made to Agnes, and he repeated it over and over again in his head so that even when it hurt so bad he wanted to bite, he never would. Never, ever would.

"I will be the best little pig in the whole world. I will be the best little pig in the whole world," he said in his head.

Over and over and over again.

Kitchen Cats

Chapter Seventeen

Learning to Listen

Kathleen called Tufts shortly after Dr. Stacey left. She explained Ozzie's problem to the receptionist, Suzanne, who was very kind.

"We can get your little guy an appointment tomorrow," she said. "But with pigs we like to have them come in the night before to get settled. You know how they are. So we may have to wait to bring him in tomorrow evening for an appointment the following morning."

Kathleen was confused. Exactly *how were* pigs, she wondered?

"I'm not sure what you mean," she said.

"They have to be anesthetized to be examined and that means they can't eat after midnight the night before," Suzanne said.

"I still don't understand," Kathleen said. "Why?"

"Well, as you know, they aren't easy to handle and they won't hold still," she replied. "And they tend to get loud when you try to make them do anything."

"But Ozzie doesn't do that," Kathleen said. "If I tell him to lie down and stay, he will."

There was silence at the other end of the phone.

"Hello?" Kathleen said.

"I can check with the doctor," Suzanne said. "My concern is that you'll bring him in, and we won't be able to do anything with him."

"I'm not concerned about that at all," Kathleen said. "Please trust me. I know my pig."

"I guess the worst thing that can happen is he has to stay the whole day and the doctors look at him the following morning," Suzanne replied. "All right, let's put him down for eight o'clock tomorrow morning."

"Thank you," Kathleen replied. "I promise he'll be fine."

She hung up the phone and called her husband at his office.

"Hey, Baby," she said. "Can you take tomorrow off from work to help me bring Ozzie up to Tufts?"

Carla was flustered. She was a smart bird and a quick study, but as hard as she tried she couldn't catch on to human talking. All kinds of noises came out of her beak, but no real words. She finally gave up. It seemed learning how to talk was a game for young crows with more flexible vocal abilities. She was going to have to leave human words to the grandchildren. Her job, it seemed, would be to figure out how to get rid of Bonnie. Her threat of sending Falstaff off to rehabilitate and then taking him to a slaughter auction was unacceptable to the old crow. Even in her retirement, Carla was a woman of action, and she never gave up until she'd tried everything. And even after she'd tried everything, she'd think of something else to try.

She hovered near the big barn that evening, keeping an eye on Bonnie. The grandchildren were on patrol, spying on the rest of the farm. The windows to the tack room were open, and Bonnie was sitting in the office chair, tapping her nails against the desktop. Carla perched on the back of the tractor, just outside the window and out of view; she knew a few spying tricks of her own.

Bonnie's cell phone rang and she answered it.

"Hello Kathleen," she said. "How's Ozzie? . . . Oh dear, that's too bad . . . You're taking him to Tufts in the morning? . . . OK . . . I can hold down the fort here. Do you think it'll take all day? . . . All right then . . . I do have a question for you. I have to give the people at the equine rehab center an answer about Falstaff . . . Ah, the money . . . I was thinking about that. Since I'm the one who rides Falstaff the most, I'd be willing to pay for his treatment. When he's sound he's a very valuable horse, which makes it worth doing for you and David . . . Yes, I know you don't see him that way . . . although most would. Horses are often investments for people . . . So your answer is definitely no, then? . . . That's fine . . . I guess we'll just have to wait and see. I know we all want what's best for Falstaff . . . yes . . . of course . . . good luck tomorrow with that sweet little pig of yours . . . goodbye . . ."

Bonnie sat quietly at her desk for a few minutes. Carla knew she was angry, as her face was a brilliant shade of scarlet. Finally, Bonnie left the office and walked up the hill to Falstaff's paddock, where she stood and stared at him. Falstaff, Captain, and James refused to raise their heads and acknowledge her. When she spoke, her words flew from her mouth like balls of spit.

"I have all day tomorrow to find a way to get you off this farm," Bonnie said. "And once I do, *I win.* I will have control over you. I . . . will . . . win."

She turned and walked purposefully back to the barn, and moments later, a solitary black crow took flight from the birch tree and slowly followed her down the hill.

"I think I have the wrong barn manager," Kathleen said.

"I *know* you have the wrong barn manager," Bo replied, pouring a cup of tea and moving a cat off a kitchen chair so she could sit down. "She always gave me a creepy feeling."

"She talks about the animals like they're objects or machines," Kathleen said. "And she seems to think what we do here is all about what the animals can do for us, not what we can do for them. It's a rescue, for goodness sakes!"

"Fire her," Bo said. "I keep saying it. If you don't want to do the job yourself, hire someone else, but get rid of her."

"I'm just not ready," Kathleen said. "I have to work. We need the money."

"It's up to you," Bo said, "but I don't trust her. What time are you leaving in the morning?"

Bo had stopped by to see Ozzie and to get last minute instructions from her mother as she was going to take care of the house animals while her parents were at Tuft's the next day.

"Really, really early," Kathleen replied.

All the arrangements for the next day were done. Bo was in charge of the house animals. Bonnie was taking care of the barns for the day. David had taken the day off from work, and Kathleen had written her stories already and e-mailed them to the office. She had checked the horse trailer to make sure the inside was nice and clean for Ozzie, then spread a thick pile of straw for him. She packed his breakfast, lunch and dinner. Once she had done everything she could think of and Bo had gone home, she went outside and sat in the mudroom with her piglet.

Ozzie had to stay closed inside the mudroom until they had a chance to build a hut for him in the garden area, and that was fine with him because he was doing his best to move as little as possible. He'd figured out the least painful way to get up and down, very slowly. If he was careful, he could roll onto his side, which was his favorite position for sleeping. Getting up was tricky, but he managed. The medicine helped a little, but Ozzie hardly cared how much it hurt. He had one goal, and that was to be a good pig.

Kathleen sat next to him and stroked the top of his head. She loved the way his hair felt both wiry and smooth at the same time.

"Do you know I'm the luckiest mama in the whole world?" she said to him. "And if I could go back in time to when Richie called and asked if we wanted you, not only would I say yes, I'd jump in the car and speed all the way up to his farm so I could get you faster. Every single minute with you is the most perfect minute in the universe. Every minute. We haven't even had you four months, and I've learned so much from you. The most important thing is never, ever take someone you love for granted for even one second. I will never, ever take you for granted, Ozzie Osboar. You are the most special little angel in the entire world, and I will do anything for you."

She sat quietly stroking his ears, and it was only a matter of a minute before Kathleen heard a voice say, "Mama, I will always do anything for you, and I promise I will be a good boy."

This time, Kathleen wasn't startled to hear a voice. She'd begun to understand something very important about her ability to communicate. If she was always busy there was no space in her brain to hear what the animals were saying. When she was a little girl and Max the German shepherd talked to her, it was easy because when she was with him, he was the only thing on her mind. Now, when she was with her animals, she was also thinking about things like what questions she'd ask on her next interview, or what she had to pick up at the grocery store for dinner. She'd forgotten how to quiet her mind and be still with her animal friends.

Today, she decided, was the day it all changed. Today she remembered why she started rescuing animals, and she promised herself she would never forget again. She leaned down and kissed Ozzie on the forehead, then settled back against the wall and listened.

Chapter Eighteen

As the Crow Flies

David and Kathleen set their alarm for four o'clock the next morning to start chores extra early. Everyone was fed and watered by five-thirty. Thankfully the truck keys were hanging on the hook where they'd left them, and by six o'clock they'd backed the horse trailer up to the side yard, and Kathleen had carefully placed Ozzie's harness on him. She explained they were going for a ride to a place where the doctors would make him better, and Ozzie followed her down the walk and through the gate. He didn't hesitate when they reached the ramp — he walked right into the trailer and stood in the straw.

"If you lie down you'll be safer," Kathleen said.

She had his favorite red plaid blanket, and she placed it on his back and gently patted him. He slowly lowered himself into the straw, looked up at his mama and smiled. Kathleen smiled back and kissed him on the nose.

"It's about an hour and a half ride to get there," she said. "Mama loves you so much, angel. We're going to get you better, whatever it takes."

She walked down the ramp, then she and David closed up the trailer and double-checked all the latches. It was time to go.

Ragano stood with his front paws on the kitchen door window and watched as they drove away. The night before, when the dogs had been let outside before bed, he'd unlatched the gate between the back and side yards, and he and Agnes had snuck over to the mudroom where they could talk to Ozzie through the screen door. It was dark outside, but the mudroom and porch lamps spilled yellow light onto the sidewalk and step.

Ozzie had slowly stood and walked to them in his stiff-legged gait.

"I'm going to the doctor's in the morning," Ozzie said.

"We heard," Ragano said. "They'll make you better, but sometimes they do things that hurt. You have to let them."

"You have to promise to be good," Agnes said. "Please promise to be good. You're my best friend in the whole world and you have to be OK."

Agnes had tears in her eyes, but Ozzie smiled.

"I'm going to do everything my Mama says," he replied. "I promise. I will be the best little pig anyone ever saw."

"I believe you will," Ragano said.

Agnes put her tiny paws up against the door, and Ozzie pressed his nose against them through the screen.

"Don't you worry about me," he said. "I'll be home soon, and I'll be good as new."

"What are you two doing?" Kathleen said from the gate. She'd opened the back door to call them inside and was surprised they weren't waiting on the step for her. "Hmmm. Have we made up from our spat? I hope so. It would be a shame if you all couldn't be friends again. We'll see what happens, but right now it's bedtime. We have a long day tomorrow. Come on, in the house."

Agnes wouldn't pry her little feet off the screen door, so Kathleen reached down and picked her up.

"He's going to come home," she said. "I promise."

And they'd all walked back around the house and went inside for the night.

It was an Indian summer day in New England. The air was unusually warm for late October, especially in the sunlight. The trees were every shade of brilliant color, and the three young crows perched in the white ash tree that towered over the driveway. They watched as Ozzie was loaded into the trailer, then they flew off to the big barn. Carla had told them Bonnie was plotting something, and they knew they had to watch every move she made that day. They didn't have a plan yet, so once they figured it out, they'd have to act fast. Carla had flown from paddock to paddock, telling all the animals what she'd heard, and they were all prepared to do whatever it took to stop Bonnie. But stop her from what? To the average person visiting Locket's Meadow that day, it would have seemed like a typical, beautiful fall day, but beneath the surface, it was anything but.

Carla left her grandchildren in charge of spying on Bonnie while she did a quick tour of the farm, checking in with everyone one more time. She made mental notes of all their skills and abilities; there was no guessing what they might need to do.

Kathleen, David and Ozzie Osboar arrived at Tufts early. Kathleen went inside to the reception area to tell them they were there.

"Oh, yes," the receptionist said. "I'm Suzanne. I spoke with you on the phone. If you can wait a few minutes I'll get some people to help you get your pig inside."

"Thank you," Kathleen said, "but I won't need any help. He'll walk with me."

The woman looked at Kathleen over the top of her glasses.

"Are you sure?" she asked. "Because we're quite used to working with pigs here, so it's no trouble."

"I'm sure," Kathleen said.

"All right," Suzanne said. "You can keep him in the trailer until we're ready for him at eight."

"Can I take him out to get some air? Is it OK if he walks around a little?"

"Walks around?" Suzanne asked. "I suppose, as long as he's under control at all times."

"Great, thanks," Kathleen said, and headed back to the trailer.

David had already opened the back gate and was sitting with Ozzie.

"We can walk him a little while we wait," Kathleen said. "They can't take him until eight o'clock."

She hooked the leash to his harness, and Ozzie slowly stood and walked down the ramp.

"Come on, sweet boy," Kathleen said. "I don't know what they're going to do to you, but I can't imagine you'll get to move around much once we get inside."

The three of them strolled onto the lawn and Ozzie poked at the grass here and there, but always stayed right next to his mama. A few minutes later a woman in a lab coat came out of the building and walked towards them.

The woman wore her long, silver hair pulled back into a ponytail and had a wide and welcoming smile.

"Hello!" she said, "I'm Dr. Paradis, and I'm examining Ozzie Osboar today."

"Good to meet you," Kathleen said. "We'll do whatever it takes to make him better. We don't care what it is."

"Of course," the vet replied.

Dr. Paradis said she needed to watch Ozzie walk, so Kathleen walked Ozzie back and forth on the lawn. As she did, more people spilled out of the building and joined the veterinarian at the edge of the parking lot.

"He certainly is goose stepping," the doctor said of his stiff-legged walk.

She introduced the rest of the people as they joined them; some were doctors and others were veterinary technicians and interns. Dr. Paradis asked Kathleen to walk Ozzie again so the entire team could evaluate his movement. Kathleen and Ozzie walked back and forth a few more times as more people poured out of the building.

"My," Kathleen said. "You certainly are attentive to pigs!"

Dr. Paradis laughed. "I don't think you understand," she said. "Most of the pigs we see here don't walk on leashes. They tend to be rather . . . unruly."

"I don't know much about most pigs," Kathleen said. "Ozzie's my first, and the other two we recently got are pretty nice, as well. Although I couldn't walk them on a leash because I don't think I could find a harness big enough for them."

The veterinarian raised one eyebrow at her.

"Alright," she said. "I think it's time we bring him inside and give him anesthesia then check his vitals and do x-rays."

"Anesthesia?" Kathleen was alarmed. "Why?"

"He's a pig," Dr. Paradis said. "They don't cooperate with examinations."

"But what do you want him to do?" Kathleen asked. "I'm sure he'll just do it."

There were a few chuckles from the onlookers.

"Well, he has to hold still," the doctor replied.

"Baby, can you get Ozzie's blanket from the trailer, please?" Kathleen asked David.

"Be right back," he said, and trotted over to get it.

"He feels more secure when he has his favorite blankie," Kathleen said.

Dr. Paradis raised her eyebrow again and waited, while the rest of the crowd grew quiet.

David returned with the red plaid blanket.

"What do you want him to do?" Kathleen asked again.

"I . . . um . . . if he could lie down on his side I can check his heart and respiration rates," she said. "If that's possible."

"Of course it's possible," Kathleen said.

She knelt down in the grass next to her pig and gently draped the fleece blanket over his back.

"Osboar, lie down," she said, patting his shoulders.

Ozzie slowly lowered his front legs, then his back legs, and only grunted a little from the pain.

"Good boy," Kathleen said. "Now roll on your side," she said, patting the side of his belly.

Ozzie slowly rolled onto his side, and Kathleen rubbed his belly. Several of the doctors and interns gasped, as did Suzanne the receptionist who had also joined them. Several of them whispered, "He listens!" and "He did it!" but Kathleen said nothing. She was focused on her pig.

"OK, I'll do this as quickly as possible," Dr. Paradis said.

"That's OK, he won't move," Kathleen said.

Nevertheless, the doctor quickly knelt next to him and put the stethoscope on Ozzie's chest. A broad smile spread across her face as she listened to his heart and lungs. When she finally removed the stethoscope from her ears, she said, "Now, that was a first!"

"What's wrong?" Kathleen asked.

"Nothing!" the doctor replied. "That was the first time I've ever listened to a pig's heart without him either being anesthetized or screaming from being pinned down. I wish everyone else could experience this!"

"He won't move if I tell him to stay," Kathleen said.

Dr. Paradis raised her eyebrow yet one more time. "OK, let's try it."

She gestured to the doctors and interns. "One at a time, please. Just be prepared to move fast if he gets up!"

"Why?" Kathleen said.

"They can bite when they're intimidated or frightened," the doctor said.

"But he never has before," Kathleen replied.

"He's never been at a clinic before," the doctor said.

Kathleen shrugged. She knew her pig, and she sat next to him as one after another squatted down and pressed their stethoscopes against Ozzie's chest.

By the time they were finished, Ozzie was dozing as Kathleen gently rubbed his belly.

"That was amazing," Dr. Paradis said. "But now we really do need to get him inside so we can anesthetize him and get started. He has to stay perfectly still for his x-rays."

"But he will stay still if I tell him," Kathleen said. "I'd rather you didn't give him anesthesia when he doesn't need it. He'll do whatever I ask."

The doctor shook her head. "There's a lot of delicate equipment in there to have a pig loose," she said. "And you won't be able to stay with him."

"But why not?" Kathleen asked. "When my daughter was little and she needed x-rays, they gave me a lead apron and let me stay in the room with her."

Dr. Paradis sighed. "It's against our protocol," she said. "You're not allowed."

"Please," Kathleen said. "I don't know why, but I just know he shouldn't be sedated. And I know he'll be a good boy and do what he's told."

The doctor looked at David.

"If my wife says Ozzie will behave," David said, "he'll behave. I've never known her to be wrong about any animal before."

"From everything I've seen I don't doubt that," the doctor said.

She crossed her arms and gazed at Ozzie, who was still lying exactly where Kathleen had put him.

"OK," she finally said. "I have to ask for special permission. It make take a while, but I'll try."

Bonnie sat at the desk in the tack room and wrote a list of all the horses on Locket's Meadow. She even included the burro, just because.

"Thirty-two horses or horse-like animals," she said. "Thirty-two." She slammed her pen down on the desk.

"She moves to the country because she wants to get a horse and six years later she has thirty-two of them," Bonnie said. "All my life I've worked with other people's horses, and I've never owned even one of my own. Not one. Who does she think she is?"

She picked up her phone and dialed.

"Hi Joe, it's Bonnie," she said. "Can I pick up that trailer around three o'clock? Right after I finish the afternoon feeding . . . yes, I'm going to get rid of that horse . . . you've seen what he does to me . . . I know, right? If you ever breathe a word of this to anyone, I will destroy your life. I know way too much about you . . . yes, you'd better believe it . . . I have a one-hour window between three and four o'clock. There aren't any lessons this afternoon, and Kathleen's daughter and her husband will both be at work. I have to get him out of here by four. They'll get back from Tufts late so they won't stop at the big barn. For all they'll know someone stole him from the farm in the middle of the night . . . yup, you're right. It does happen. Have the trailer ready and I'll get it back to you as soon as I drop him off at the horse traders . . . yes, he's a big horse so he's worth about $600 by the pound, and I'm splitting it with you . . . OK, bye . . ."

Bonnie hung up the phone.

"I think *thirty-one* horses is enough for any one woman," she said, crossing a name off her list, then crossing her arms and looking out the window as one lone crow sped past.

The Tufts doctors had gone back into the building, but several of the vet techs stayed behind to rub Ozzie's belly. Kathleen had finally realized her pig might not be like other pigs at all, with all the fuss everyone made over him. But she still refused to be distracted; she'd decided the night before that all her attention was going to be on Ozzie, and nothing else mattered.

One of the vet techs led them inside the building and showed them to a small stall where Ozzie would wait. She told them where the lounge was so they could relax and have a cup of coffee, but Kathleen told her they would stay with their pig.

"I can't leave him alone in a strange place," Kathleen said.

"I'll go get coffee and bring it back," David said.

It was already nine-thirty and they still didn't know if Kathleen would be allowed to assist with x-rays. She had no idea why, but she knew it was important that her pig be awake while the doctors worked on him. She covered Ozzie with his blanket and he lowered himself to his belly. Then Kathleen sat next to him in the clean pine shavings, rubbed his soft ears, and waited.

Chapter Nineteen

It's a Plan

"Grandmother!" shrieked Carlita. "Grandmother!"
She landed next to Carla on Harriet and Ice's gate.
"We know the plan! We know the plan!" Carlita shouted.

"Where are your brothers?" Carla asked.

"I told them to stay behind and keep spying," Carlita said. "Just in case something changes."

"Smart girl," Carla said. "Has anyone ever told you you're a lot like your grandmother?"

Carlita beamed. "Just you," she said.

"One day I'll tell you stories about when I was a little girl. Don't ever tell this to anyone . . . your father got his spunk from his mother! But this is no time to talk about genetics," Carla said briskly. "Tell me what's happening so we can organize a counter attack."

Carlita quickly told her everything she'd heard Bonnie say, some of it in human as she'd become quite good at memorizing lots of words quickly.

"So, between three and four o'clock she's planning to load Falstaff and take him away," Carla said. "And we need to find a way to stop her. Not so easy."

"Can't we just block the driveway?" Carlita asked.

"With what?" Carla asked.

"Well, I don't know about anyone else here," Harriet said from the pile of straw in the shed, "but Sister and I can block a whole lot of driveway."

"Why yes, Sister," Ice chimed in. "Wouldn't it be nice to take a stroll across the farm this afternoon?"

"But how will you get there?" Carla asked.

"When you lived in the cages for as long as we did," Ice said, "the latch on a paddock gate is a rather simple task."

Ice stood up and gave a mighty shake, sending a shower of bright, yellow straw into the air around her. She lumbered to the gate, stood on her hind legs, set her front feet against the fence post, then lifted the gate latch up and over. She dropped back to the ground and the gate swung open.

"We practiced in case we had to make an escape," Harriet said, joining her sister. "Because you never know."

"You never know," Ice repeated.

"Perfect!" Carla said. "Now we just need to get everyone else out."

"You don't worry about that," Ice said.

"We can take care of this side of the farm if you take care of the rest," Harriet said. "After all, the more the merrier!"

"I'll let you know when Bonnie's left to get the trailer," Carla said. "Come Carlita, we have to get organized next door."

There was a loud rustle in the brown leaves of the ash tree alongside the pigs' paddock, and another pair of crows dropped down and landed on the fence alongside them.

"Oh, mother," Carl said. "Tsk, tsk, tsk. What have you been up to?"

"I told you, Carl," Wilson said. "No good. She's been up to no good. And without us!"

"Oh dear," Carl said. "All our years of preparing for something as great and noble as this, and you hide it from us? Mother! How could you? And what do you mean I got my spunk from you?'"

But Carl was smiling, and Carla smiled back.

"The more, the merrier," Carla said. "It's a big driveway to block. Let's get started!"

It was nearly noon and David and Kathleen dozed as they waited with Ozzie in the pine shavings.

Finally, they heard someone say, "Hello," from above. They opened their eyes and saw Suzanne smiling down.

"It's time for Ozzie's x-rays," she said. "I can show you where to go."

They stood up and Kathleen hooked Ozzie's leash to his harness.

"Let's go, Osboar," she said.

They followed Suzanne through the maze of stalls and into a wide hallway that was covered with rubber matting. It was very long, and Kathleen worried that Ozzie would be tired and sore by the time they got to the x-ray room at the far end, but he slowly walked next to his mother's right heel, back legs stiff, determinedly moving one foot in front of the other. As they passed each open doorway people turned to stare and Kathleen smiled back at them. If they had never seen a well-behaved pig before, she thought, it was probably about time they did. They paused to have Ozzie step onto a floor scale. He weighed eighty pounds.

"No wonder it's too hard to pick you up, whee piggy piggy!" Kathleen said.

Just past the scale they turned a corner into a large room with a big x-ray machine in the center. There was a technician's booth and blue mats on the floor exactly like the ones in a high school gymnasium. Dr. Paradis entered through a doorway at the far end of the room.

"I'm sorry it took so long," she said, "but it's not easy to get permission to break the rules, and it's even harder to locate all the people who have to sign off on it to make it happen. But we're ready!"

One of the technicians handed Kathleen a long, heavy, lead apron.

"We only have permission for one person to be in the room with him," the doctor said to David, "so you can wait in the booth if you'd like to watch. I'd rather you stay near in case your wife needs help."

"I'll watch, but I doubt she'll need help," he said, and walked over to the booth.

A technician came out and showed Kathleen where Ozzie needed to lie down so they could get the correct picture of his spine.

"The problem," said Dr. Paradis, "is we need to place one of these plates directly beneath him to get the picture and it has to be positioned exactly right."

"That's not a problem," Kathleen said. "Where does the plate go and where does the pig go?"

They described what they wanted for the first x-ray.

"Ready, Ozzie?" Kathleen asked.

Her pig had been standing perfectly still alongside her. He looked up at his mama and smiled.

"Mama!" he said. "Mama, Mama!"

Dr. Paradis looked at Kathleen, then shook her head.

"Some things I can believe," she said, "but some are just a little too much for me."

"Right here, Ozzie," Kathleen said.

She didn't care if anyone believed her pig could talk, or bark, or stay perfectly still. She didn't care if at the end of the day she and her little family left and the people at Tufts convinced themselves it had been one, long, bizarre hallucination. She only cared that Ozzie got better. She lined him up exactly where they wanted him and then patted his back so he would lie down. He slowly dropped to his stomach, and she set the plate alongside him. Then she patted his belly so he rolled neatly onto his side and onto the plate.

"Almost," the tech said. "Can you move him so the plate is an inch further this way?" she pointed.

"I can move the plate," Kathleen said. "He won't mind."

Everyone stepped back.

"It may pinch him," the doctor said.

"He won't mind," Kathleen repeated. "Easy Ozzie," she said as she slid the plate beneath him.

He grunted, but she patted his belly.

"We got this, Ozzie Bear," she said.

"That's it!" the tech said. "Don't let him move!"

Everyone scattered to their places behind the walls, but Kathleen sat next to Ozzie as the x-ray machine buzzed.

"Perfect!" the doctor said. "Now we have to get the plate under this section of his back."

She showed Kathleen where the next area was, but it was too far away from the first spot to try to slide the plate beneath the heavy animal.

"Come on Ozzie, time to stand up," Kathleen said. "We have to move you."

Ozzie slowly rose to his feet.

"I'm sorry, angel," she said. "I know you're sore, but we have to put you in a different spot."

She kissed him on his soft nose and moved him over a few inches before asking him to lie down again. Ozzie did exactly as she asked and Dr. Paradis nodded her approval of his position. The staff scattered, and Kathleen again heard the buzz of the machine.

"OK," Dr. Paradis said. "Here's where the next one has to go."

Kathleen and Ozzie maneuvered around until it was just right.

Buzz!

Dr. Paradis popped back out.

"We still need one more, and you've reached your limit on how many times you can be in here while we film," she said. "We can give him a quick acting sedative that will wear off fast so we can get the last one."

"No!" Kathleen said. "Please let me stay. I don't care."

"I'm sorry," Dr. Paradis said. "But there are some rules we can't bend."

Kathleen sat down and rubbed her pig's belly. He hadn't moved since she'd put him in his last position.

"Please," she said. "If we set him up and I tell him to stay, he won't move even if I leave the room. I don't want him sedated."

The doctor looked doubtful.

"If you leave and he jumps up and starts to move around the room, there's some very delicate equipment in here . . ."

"I'll stand right behind that wall," Kathleen said. "And I promise he won't move. You'll be a good boy, won't you, Osboar? The doctors need one more picture so they have everything they need to fix you up."

Ozzie looked up at his mama and smiled.

"All right, fine," Dr. Paradis said. "But just one try, and that's it!"

"That's all we need," Kathleen said. "Where does he need to be?"

The doctor showed her what they needed a picture of and where he had to be positioned. Kathleen got Ozzie up yet one more time and moved him into his last position.

"Perfect," Dr. Paradis said.

"Ozzie, you stay," Kathleen said. "I'm going to leave the room for just a few seconds and then I'll be right back."

She looked up at the technician behind the window.

"Ready?" she asked.

"Go!" the tech said, and Kathleen stood up and walked behind the wall as quickly as the heavy lead apron would allow. She couldn't see her pig on the other side, but moments later she heard the buzz and she peeked around the corner. Ozzie hadn't moved a muscle.

"Now that," said Dr. Paradis, "is one very good pig. He's a rock star!"

She stooped down to give him a pat, then looked up at the pair of techs.

"Can one of you hold his leash while I take his parents into the next room and we see what we got?" she asked.

Both techs rushed over, smiling. One of them took Ozzie's leash while the other bent down to rub his belly.

Dr. Paradis led Kathleen and David into the next room, which was filled with people in white lab coats, sitting at desks studying images on their computer screens.

"Over here, doctor," one of them said. "Look at this."

The two of them bent over the screen and spoke in a whisper. Everyone in the room wore a somber expression, and Kathleen held David's hand, growing more afraid by the second. Finally, Dr. Paradis called them over.

"This is the last picture we took," she said. "Look right here."

She pointed to a spot where Ozzie's spine was bent at a slight angle.

"Do you see that line right there?" the doctor asked. "It runs right through here."

David and Kathleen leaned in and looked where she had traced her finger on the screen. They both nodded.

"That's a break in his vertebrae," Dr. Paradis said. "He has a broken back. The muscles in a pig's back are so incredibly strong and tough they can hold the break together for him, which is why he's alive and walking even as well as he is."

She paused and looked Kathleen right in the eye.

"I don't know how you knew," she said, "But . . . if we had given him general anesthesia it would have relaxed the muscles in his back completely, they would have stopped holding the break together, and we would have lost him."

Ernie

Chapter Twenty

Just Desserts

"Please hurry," Kathleen said. "I feel like we need to get home as quickly as possible."

Suzanne was printing out the paperwork that described Ozzie's visit and his diagnosis. The veterinarians said there was nothing they could do for a broken back aside from keeping him in a small enclosure so he wouldn't reinjure himself, while Mother Nature did her job of healing. They suggested two months in a very small area, and after that Ozzie could move to a bigger pen. They said he might never walk any better than he currently did, but he *could* walk, and that's what counted.

It had taken forever for Dr. Paradis to write up the report, and it was now two o'clock. Kathleen wanted to get Ozzie home and settled in after his long day. He was already in the trailer, snuggled under his red plaid blanket in the big pile of straw, and David was waiting with him.

"He really is a very good pig," Suzanne said as she handed her the completed paperwork to sign. "Nobody can stop talking about him."

"He's a rock star," Kathleen said. She signed the last page and handed the copy back to her. "He was born that way."

She picked up her stack of paperwork, said good-by and raced to the truck.

"Let's go," she said to David. "I'm worried and I don't know why. You drive — I need to think."

They climbed into the truck and were on their way.

The ladies of the little barn were nervous about breaking out of their paddock and going over to the big barn. All of them, that is, except for Cressida, who was notorious for some very impressive breakouts in her younger days. She was chomping at the bit, anxious for a chance to race around the farm. Calypso tried to convince her that this was a very serious situation and she needed to be part of the team, but Cressida knew if the opportunity presented itself, she'd take it. Calypso hoped the opportunity wouldn't present until after their work was done.

Locket, meanwhile, was working on her own part of the plan. She was the only one who could communicate with Michael, the farm ghost, whose talent for opening gates was legendary and had helped them many times in the past. She wandered off into a corner of the paddock and concentrated.

Classy stayed near Harriet and Ice and helped them design the quickest, most efficient way to turn loose several paddocks filled with animals. They decided the best way to do it was to open all the gates much earlier, and everyone would remain inside until the signal was given, when they were to meet behind the indoor arena.

The crows had gathered in the haymow, which had become home base, to discuss timing and strategy.

"This would be an excellent time to have some pigeons on the farm, wouldn't you say, Carl?" Wilson asked, remembering a previous adventure they'd been involved in when they were younger.

"Alas, we have none," Wilson said, "and no time to round any up. We'll have to make do with what we have. Crows are also pretty good at this revenge business, you know."

"The way I see it," Carla said, "timing is most important."

"Yes," Carl said. "But that's if we can get all the animals out and ready to gather as soon as she loads Falstaff in the trailer. And there isn't a lot of room to hide them near the bottom of the driveway. We can't fit more than a dozen horses in the yard behind the little house."

Bo and Craig's cottage was very small, but it was the only hiding place they had where the driveway needed to be blocked.

"What about the indoor arena?" Wilson said. "She has no reason to look in there, nor will she have time if she has only one hour to pick up a trailer, load a horse and get off the farm again."

"Good idea," Carla said.

The three young crows watched the grown-ups with awe. They'd heard stories about their father and Wilson and the exploits of their youth, but they never thought they'd witness it first-hand, and they certainly couldn't have imagined their grandmother being involved. The young crows had gotten into so much trouble plotting their escapades, and now here they were, being woven into an intricate plot to rescue a horse from a kidnapping. They couldn't have been prouder of their family or more excited for themselves.

Finally, the crows had the last details sewn up.

"Everyone knows what they're doing?" Carla asked.

"Yes ma'am," the crows replied.

"Get out and spread the word," Carla said.

"Not so fast," said a voice from the open haymow door. "What's going on here?"

The children turned their heads and gasped. Carl tried to speak but only managed to produce a sputtering sound.

"Bettina!" Wilson said. "Delighted to see you as always!"

"Wilson," replied the children's mother, "I wish I could say the same for you. But . . . I can't. I overheard enough. I don't mind the children doing a little harmless spying, but being involved in a plot to stop a kidnapping sounds way too dangerous for them. I'm afraid I have to ground them to the tree during this operation."

"But Mom!" the young crows cried out. "Nooooo!"

"You can get hurt," Bettina said. "I think the adults can take care of this on their own. I'll take over and do whatever the children were supposed to do. I certainly don't want to see anything happen to Falstaff, either."

"Dearest," Carl said. "You can't possibly do their job. No one else can."

"Excuse me?" Bettina replied. "Are you saying I'm incompetent?"

"Not at all," Carl said. "And if you can speak human, you are more than welcome to take over for them."

"Speak human?" Bettina said. "Why would I be able to speak human?"

"Carlita, say something," Carla said.

"Ummm . . . 'no, no Mama'?" Carlita said.

"Better than that," Carla said.

"I . . . uh . . ." Carlita was a little intimidated by her mother, but she finally managed to say, "No, no, bad dog! Don't poop on my floor. Go outside!"

Bettina's beak dropped open.

"As you can see," Wilson said, "you don't know how to speak human, but your children do, and since we don't have time to come up with another plan, we have to get started."

Bettina continued to stare with her beak wide open.

"OK," Carl said. "Let's go!"

If any humans had been watching, they would have seen a half-dozen crows zip out through the haymow door and race off in every direction of the farm. A seventh crow, who seemed a little dazed and confused, flew out of the barn much more slowly, then settled on the crest of the barn roof, where she perched for quite a while.

"We are definitely lost," David said. "I have no idea how to get back to the highway."

"Why would they detour us then not tell us where to detour to?" Kathleen asked, not expecting an answer.

There had been an accident on Interstate 91 and the state police had closed the road and directed traffic off the highway, but once they were on the side roads the best they could do was guess at which way to go. They tried to follow the roads that seemed to run parallel to the highway, but they soon lost sight of it.

"Can we please stop and ask for directions?" Kathleen asked.

"Not yet," David said. "I can figure this out."

Kathleen closed her eyes. She was trying not to worry, but every time she thought about the farm she felt panicked. She kept feeling that Falstaff was in danger, and she had no idea why.

Why? She tried to relax and calm her mind, but it wasn't easy. She was worried about Ozzie and worried about being away from the farm and worried about being worried. She decided to think instead about what a good boy Ozzie had been that day. Over and over, she remembered how he followed directions and was a perfect little angel pig. She was so proud of him. She pictured him unloading off the trailer when they got home and walking back into the mudroom, snuggling on his bed and waiting for his belly rub. It was the most relaxing part of the day for her, and she felt herself sink back into her seat. And then . . . out of nowhere . . . she had a vision of Falstaff standing in line outside a slaughterhouse, waiting in a long line of horses for his turn to file inside.

She sat bolt upright.

"Stop at the next gas station and ask for directions!" she shouted at David.

"What is the matter with you?" David said. "Don't yell at me! I'm hauling a trailer, here. It's not that easy!"

"Something's wrong with Falstaff," Kathleen replied. "I just know it."

"So call Bonnie and tell her to check on him," David replied.

"I can't," she replied. "I think Bonnie is what's wrong with him."

Bonnie finished feeding the horses at precisely three o'clock. She'd seen Bo drive away moments earlier to head to her late shift at work, and she knew Craig wouldn't be home from work until after four o'clock, so she decided to finish cleaning the barn later and jumped in her truck to get the trailer and bring it back. She'd already put Falstaff in a stall so she could grab him and load quickly.

Captain had seen Bonnie walking up the hill to get Falstaff.

"What if the plan doesn't work?" Captain had said. "Run her over and get out of here!"

"I trust everyone," Falstaff said. "If I don't do my part Bonnie won't get caught and then we'll all be in danger, all the time."

Captain knew Falstaff was right, but he was terrified for his friend.

Captain and James waited quietly in their paddock. Five minutes passed. Then ten. Then fifteen. Nothing happened. And then . . . the boys heard a gate latch open at the bottom of the hill. Then another closer to them. Then the next one on the way up. No one was in sight, yet the latches kept dropping.

"Happy early Halloween, boys," Captain said.

Finally, the latch to their gate came undone, and the gate swung inwards towards them, but they stood and waited. The last paddock at the top of the hill was Ernie and Star's, the two biggest drafts. They waited to hear the rattle of their latch, but there was nothing. The gate shook a few times, then all was quiet. Captain walked to the fence near Ernie's gate and looked. The draft boys had recently broken their latch and it hadn't been fixed. The one thing Michael the barn ghost couldn't open was an elastic bungee cord, which was exactly what held their gate closed.

David had finally found his way back onto the highway and they were headed in the right direction. They still had about forty minutes to go before they'd arrive home, and that was only if they didn't hit traffic. Kathleen was sure she was losing her mind. Why on earth would Bonnie do something to hurt Falstaff? It made no sense. But then she thought about how every horse Bonnie rode came home injured or sore. That made no sense, either. Nothing made sense. She hoped she was wrong and that when they got back to the farm all would be perfectly normal, and they would unload Ozzie and settle down for a nice, quiet evening of belly rubs. Still, she anxiously watched the road ahead for signs of traffic delays, hoping there would be none.

The crows bustled around the farm, checking details and making sure everything was going according to plan. Carl and Wilson flew up the hill to check the gates and found the bungee cord on Ernie and Star's paddock.

"Oh man," Wilson said. "That's not good."

"How are we gonna get them out?" Carl said.

Theirs was the only paddock with electric wire fencing because the boys had broken so many fence boards David had grown tired of replacing them. The electric wire around the top kept the horses away from the boards, but now they had no way to get out.

"They're the biggest horses we have," Wilson said. "We need them."

Ernie eyed the electric fence wire. He didn't like it; neither of the big boys did. It was very unpleasant to be shocked by it.

"How high can you jump?" Wilson asked.

"Don't worry about us," Ernie said. "We'll figure this out. Get back to work."

The crows flew off, leaving the big drafts to deal with the electric wire and the closed gate.

When Carla gave the signal, Harriet and Ice had let themselves out of their pen, and they and the other animals from behind the little farmhouse slowly filed down the path towards the indoor riding arena. They quietly walked along the south side, then entered the open double doors at the west end. The horses from the paddocks at the top of the hill came down to the little house and huddled behind it. It would have been suspicious to have empty paddocks at the bottom of the hill near the barn, so the horses in the lower fields would wait until Bonnie had loaded Falstaff and gotten into the truck. Then they'd race down the hill and join their friends.

The entire farm was ready to go by three-thirty. Time ticked past slowly as the crows silently crisscrossed the farm, constantly checking every detail. The crows could tell by the angle of the sun it was closing in on four o'clock, and they finally heard the sound of a diesel engine turning into the driveway, followed by the crash of a trailer rolling over the speed bump at the entrance to the farm. It was time.

Ragano had been watching for Bonnie's truck at the front window. He was waiting until the very last second to join the others. As soon as he heard the truck pass the house he sprang into action.

"That's it!" he shouted to Agnes. "She's back!"

He raced to the back door, stood on his hind legs, wrapped a paw around the knob and pulled. It took a half-dozen tries, but he finally got it open. The dogs raced into the yard and Ragano leaped over the fence. Agnes, however, was stopped at the gate.

"Go ahead, Ragano!" she said. "I'll catch up."

She quickly found a patch of soft dirt in the zinnia bed and began to tunnel under the fence as fast as her little paws could dig.

Ragano ran down the path and joined the animals waiting in the indoor arena. He quickly found Locket and stood next to her.

"Hey, Locket!" Ragano said. "We're on an adventure!"

"I once swore I'd never leave my paddock again," Locket replied, "and I certainly hope this is the very last time I have to."

"If we can get rid of Bonnie," Ragano said, "maybe this will be the last time. Once she's gone, we won't have anything to worry about."

"I think once this is over and Falstaff's safe, I will tell you some stories about things that have happened on this farm," Locket said. "The battle of good versus evil never seems to end."

Carlita swooped through the doorway and landed on Locket's back.

"She's leading him out right now!" she said. "Get ready!"

They heard Falstaff's huge feet clunking up the metal ramp followed by the loud slam of the trailer gates. The tension was unbearable. Moments later, the engine started.

"Now!" Carlita yelled.

The truck shifted into gear and the horses, pigs, and goats rushed to the south end of the barn and trotted out onto the driveway. The horses that had hidden behind the little house were already blocking the bottom, and those in the lower paddocks came clattering down the hill, racing past Bonnie's truck and joining the dozens of animals already in place. They stood silent and still. Ragano stood in front with Locket, Classy, Cressida, and Calypso. Behind them were Captain and James, then Beatrice, Benny, Bingo, Bart, and all the rest of the rescues. Bonnie pulled the trailer to within a few feet of them, then leaned on the horn and held it. Not a single animal flinched.

She got out of the truck.

"Get out of my way, you stupid animals!" She picked up a rock and threw it at Locket. Ragano crouched low and growled.

"Go! Get out!" she ran at them waving her arms, yelling at the top of her lungs. She picked up a stick and waved it at Classy.

The two huge sows pushed forward and stood in front of the Arab. Their eyes were narrowed and bits of white foam dripped from the corners of their mouths.

Bonnie knew nothing about pigs, and she took a step back.

"You're nothing but a big pile of ham and bacon," she screamed at them. "Get out of here! I have to leave now! Go!"

She waved her arms at them and stomped her feet. Carla sensed she was beginning to panic. "Now!" she called to her grandchildren.

Carlyle swooped in and circled Bonnie's head.

"No, no, bad dog! Don't poop on my floor. Go outside!" he shouted at her. "No, no, bad dog! Don't poop on my floor. Go outside!"

"What?!" Bonnie screamed. "Go away!"

She picked up a stick and swung it at him, but he effortlessly dodged her.

Carlos dove down next.

"You nasty, rotten, stupid, fat, lazy, ugly piece of turd," Carlos said. "I will teach you a lesson you will never forget!"

Bonnie gasped and turned a brilliant shade of scarlet. She grabbed a second stick and swung both at the crow.

"YOU WILL LEARN!" Carlos screeched, "Or I will find a way to ship you to a slaughter yard and turn you into dog food!"

Bonnie had clearly recognized her own words coming from the mouth of a crow.

"I . . . I . . . I wasn't going to do it!" she cried out. "I didn't mean it! It was a joke!"

She dropped the sticks and backed up against the grill of her truck.

"I was only kidding . . .," she stammered.

Carlita dove down towards her face, and Bonnie screamed at the top of her lungs.

"YOU WILL LEARN!" Carlita shouted at her, "Or I will find a way to ship you to a slaughter yard and turn you into dog food!"

Bonnie screamed again. "No! I didn't do anything!"

"I WILL BREAK YOU!" Carlita screamed, and her brothers joined her as they circled her head and the three chanted, "I WILL BREAK YOU!"

Bonnie put her hands over her face as they darted closer and closer to her.

"I'm not afraid of any of you!" Bonnie shouted. "I'm not! Let's see how you feel about getting run over with a truck!"

She clung to the side of her truck as she worked her way towards the driver's side door. She climbed in and revved the engine.

"Get out of my way now or you're all road kill!"

The animals inched backwards.

"Yeah, I thought so," Bonnie shouted, and began to inch forward. "It's a biiiiiig truck!"

David and Kathleen rounded the corner of Rainbow Road and turned onto Old Litchfield Turnpike.

"Finally!" Kathleen said. "Almost there! Don't pull into the driveway; just stop at the bottom of the hill so you don't have to back out again. I'll lead Ozzie out of the trailer and walk him up to the house."

David pulled up to the side of the road at the bottom of the driveway and Kathleen looked up towards the barn.

"Holy cats!" she shouted. "I just saw Agnes run down the path! How did she get out? You bring Ozzie in. I'll get Aggie!"

Kathleen jumped out of the truck and ran up the driveway towards the path to the big barn. The grass and brush was taller than her head so she couldn't see where her dog had gone. She heard a horse scream, and then terrible cracking noises from the top of the hill near Ernie's paddock and she ran faster.

Bonnie revved the engine one more time.

"That's my last warning!" she screamed. "I'm done with you stupid brats!"

She shifted the truck into gear, but just then they heard a loud commotion at the top of hill . . . horses screaming, the crashing and cracking of wood followed by the clattering of enormous feet racing down the driveway. The animals blocking Bonnie stopped backing away. Bonnie looked in her side view mirror and choked. Barreling towards her was Ernie, followed by Star. Before she could take her foot off the brake pedal, Ernie had skid to a stop alongside the engine of her truck, turned on his haunches and BOOM! He double barreled both of his gigantic back hooves into the side of her truck. The hood popped open and steam escaped. BOOM! He slammed into the truck again and the passenger door came unhinged and hung loose. BOOM! One last time and the right front tire exploded and the front end of the truck dropped to the ground.

There was a moment of silence before Bonnie opened her door. She walked around the front of her crumpled truck, glaring at the animals in the driveway. She reached Ernie, looked him in the eye, made a fist of her hand, drew it back, and punched him in the neck with all her might.

At that moment, Agnes had finally reached the scene. Before Bonnie could finish pulling her arm back from punching Ernie, Agnes leaped into the air and bit Bonnie's wrist as hard as she could, then wouldn't let go of her jacket sleeve. Bonnie brought her left arm back and made a fist to punch Agnes and Ragano leaped into the air and chomped down on it.

Kathleen had exited the path near the indoor arena just as Bonnie hit Ernie. She ran to the driveway with what breath she had left while Ragano and Agnes hung from Bonnie's waving arms.

"Leave it!" she shouted at her dogs as she got there, and they let go and dropped to the ground.

Kathleen looked at the trailer.

"Falstaff!" she called, and he whinnied back to her from inside.

She breathed a deep sigh of relief.

"You hit my horse," Kathleen said to Bonnie, gasping for breath. "It's expressly against the contract you signed. You're . . . fired."

Bonnie stood next to her ruined truck, expressionless, and without a sound the animals slowly dispersed, walking back to their paddocks.

Except for Cressida, of course, who reared up on her hind legs, whinnied at the top of her lungs, and tore up the driveway at top speed.

Ernie and Star walked up the hill behind her.

"Wow," Ernie said. "That electric fence smarts."

"No kidding," Star sighed.

Harriet, David, and Ice

Chapter Twenty-One

Ever After

It was early October, almost exactly one year later. The sun had set and a huge, pumpkin-orange moon hung low in the eastern sky. Kathleen had worked most of the day and was just finishing up. Her morning had been filled with appointments in which she met with people who wanted to communicate with their animals. It turned out that once she finally remembered how to hear animals there was no stopping their voices. She decided to start a business helping other people understand what their animals were saying. In the afternoon, she'd spent several hours working on a new book she was writing, and that evening was spent teaching people with special needs how to ride horses. She no longer worked at the newspaper. She'd decided she needed to be more available to her animals and had found a way to earn enough income while focusing on the things that most mattered to her.

She and Ragano, her assistant instructor, finished teaching their lessons, and she asked Olivia, one of the volunteer barn girls, to lead Calypso back to the small barn. Kathleen untacked Falstaff, gave him some mints and led him into his stall for the night. Falstaff, along with all of the other horses, was as fit as a fiddle. In fact, all of the lame horses were miraculously healed the day after Bonnie left the farm for good.

Kathleen had just closed Falstaff's stall when Olivia came running back into the barn.

"Pigs are loose next door!" she said.

"Again?" Kathleen sighed. "OK, let's get the rest of these horses put away, and then we'll deal with them. The pigs won't go anywhere."

A few minutes later, all the horses were in their stalls, and Kathleen and her young volunteers walked down the moonlit path. They cut through the little white barn, walked out the other side and there, beneath the moonlight, was a sight to behold.

The yard was filled with loose animals, all of them drenched in yellow moonlight. So many new rescues had arrived in the past year, including sheep from the agricultural school that were being sent to slaughter, alpacas from a farm that had closed down, and a small round black pig named Iris Magnolia rescued from a slaughterhouse on Long Island. All of them were milling around in the yard, alternately frolicking and nibbling at grass. Most prominent of all were the two large sows, Harriet and Ice, who had pushed through the fence to gorge on fruit that had dropped from the pear tree.

"You guys keep an eye on the animals while I figure out how they got loose this time," Kathleen said, and eight young teenagers ran through the gate and joined the frolicking animals.

It was irresistible, really . . . animals dancing in the moonlight couldn't be left to dance alone. Kathleen wished she could join them, but first she had to find the broken fence. Ragano followed at her heel as she waded through the sheep and goats, then walked past the little black pig and gave her a pat. The many locks and latches on the sows' gate had held, but apparently the perfume of ripe pears was more than Harriet and Ice could endure. Kathleen found the broken boards where the ladies had escaped. As usual, if the ladies were out, they made sure their friends came out with them, and the other gates had been opened.

Kathleen hiked down to the garage to get new fence boards, a hammer and the bucket of nails. She couldn't help but smile as the children raced around with the animals, laughing and singing. As the moon rose higher in the sky it changed from orange to yellow and then to a brilliant silver, washing over the laughing animals and children, drenching everything with the glow of magic.

Wood clunked against wood, and hammer whacked against nails as Kathleen repaired the fence. She kept an eye on the moonlit dancers while she worked, and when she finished she paused and watched for a while. The alpacas stretched their elegant necks up into the trees to pick off the fall leaves, while the sheep and goats raced the children back and forth across the lawn. Iris Magnolia joined Harriet and Ice beneath the pear tree, slurping up soft fruit and smacking her lips.

Finally, some of the parents arrived to pick up their children, and Kathleen announced it was time put the animals in their stalls and paddocks and go home. There were cries of protest, but everyone helped lead the truant farm residents to their various sheds and pens. They all danced until the very end, and even the cleanup of the impromptu party became part of the magic.

The very last to return to their pen were the founders of the festival, Harriet and Ice. The pear bonanza was hard to leave, but, with a little prompting from Ragano, they finally lumbered up the hill and into their shed, where they quickly fluffed their bedding and prepared for the night. All the gates were locked, the children dispersed and the barn lights turned off.

Kathleen let Agnes out the back door. She ran to the little paddock that used to be the vegetable garden and raced in circles around the pink pig standing at the gate. They played for a few minutes while Kathleen warmed a fleece blanket in the dryer. Ragano jumped over the fence and ran through the barn to see his best friend.

"Locket!" he called, and she came to the fence. "Do you see the moon tonight? Mama says it's the most magical moon she's ever seen!"

"Yes," Locket said. "I think it's quite beautiful."

"I believe in magic," Ragano said.

"We have to believe in it on this farm," Locket said. "It's how we survive."

"Are the horses going to dance tonight?" Ragano asked.

"I'm sure they will," Locket said. "I'm going to stay here and be quiet for a while. If you have a few minutes, I'd like to tell you a story I've been saving."

"I have time!" Ragano said. "Mama still has to night-night Ozzie. What's the story about?"

"It's the story of a very special duck who used to live on the farm," Locket said. "He's buried right under the rock you use to jump out of the yard. I've been saving it for a night just like tonight . . ."

Back in the yard, Kathleen picked up Agnes and brought her into the house, then took a warm fleece blanket out of the dryer and brought it outside to Ozzie's pen.

"Time to go to sleep," she said.

She stopped at his gate that led into the yard and fastened the latch. The ladies had opened it, but Ozzie stayed inside. He'd promised more than a year ago that he'd always be a very, very good pig, and he had never broken his vow. Instead, he had watched everyone and smiled, knowing his mama was going to be home soon, and they would have their special time. He walked into his little hut, still slightly stiff in his hind legs as he always would be, and Kathleen crawled in next to him and placed the warm blanket over his back. Then she gently patted him until he lay down in the straw and flopped over onto his side.

"There we go," his mama said. "I will tell you a story before you fall asleep."

She rubbed his belly and Ozzie made his happy grunt, because it was always the same story every, single night, and it was his favorite.

"Once upon a time there was a tiny piglet named Ozzie Osboar, and he lived on a farm called Locket's Meadow," she said. "He had a mama and his mama had him and they loved each other very, very much. He was so little that his mama could lift him up hiiiiigh in the air and say, 'Whee! Piggy piggy piggy!' and he would giggle and wiggle and they had so much fun together, that mama and her piggy . . ." Kathleen rubbed his belly and said, "Wheee piggy piggy piggy!" and they both closed their eyes and remembered their blissful yesterdays while being perfectly grateful for that moment now that he was all grown up and snuggled under his red plaid blanket.

The silver moon slowly slid across the velvet sky and the farm quietly listened to the sounds of stories being told while the horses readied for a night of dancing under the full moon. Another day on Locket's Meadow had come to a close. Tomorrow was a mystery. But at that exact moment, everything was exactly perfect, and that's all that would ever matter.

Mama tucking Ozzie in for a nap, Spring 2014

Epilogue of a Love Story

When Ozzie Osboar came into my life everything changed instantly. I was madly in love, and remain so to this day. My Ozzie is no longer with us, as he died on Black Friday in 2014, which he thought was pretty funny (his namesake Ozzy Osbourn is in the band *Black Sabbath.* Haha.) While Ozzie was never very healthy, he had a heart filled with love, especially for his mama, and I will forever count myself as the luckiest mama in the entire world.

I am also, without a doubt, one of the laziest writers in the world, and I seldom have an original idea. All of the Locket's Meadow books are based on actual events, but from the point of view of our animals. Since I'm a medium and an animal communicator, my writing process goes like this — I sit at the computer, ask them to give me their words, then start to type. This book, however, was different. I'd started it several years ago, while Ozzie and many of the other characters were still alive. I didn't know at the time why I put it aside, but apparently, the animals did. I was doing it wrong.

Early in 2016, Ozzie began harassing me to finish his story (remember that I can hear animals who have died, as well,) so I started back to work on it in June, beginning with Ozzie's arrival, followed by Harriet and Ice, etc. I kept hitting a wall, so I decided to have a "conference call" with my book characters, both those who were alive and those who had crossed over. They told me they wanted more leeway in how the story was told — rather than sticking to events, they wanted to write it so readers would truly understand the dangers of being a farm animal in today's world. I said I'd give it a try, and the story quickly began to flow.

I'd never written anything before that left me hanging at the end of each day, wondering what in the world could possibly happen next. I'd beg my animal sources to tell me where I would start the next morning and they would tell me to chill. The suspense was terrible, both for me and for my husband, David, who was reading along as I was writing. By the last few chapters, I was just as surprised as anyone at the turn of events, and if I were the one in charge it would have had an entirely different twist. However, when all was said and done, I saw the wisdom in the way my friends chose to tell the story, and the integrity of their characters remained intact.

What is real in this story? Everything about Ozzie, from his arrival on the farm, to making his promise to Agnes, to being such a good boy at Tufts that his life was spared. Everything. Also, the story of Harriet and Ice is true, and yes, as I write this, those old girls are still here and still have a knack for opening gates. Ragano's story is also quite real, and he sat next to me every moment of writing this book. During the process he carefully hid the fact that he had a malignant tumor growing on his spine, and he didn't show any symptoms until several weeks after I'd finished the first draft. Shortly after, I lost one of the other great loves of my life when Ragano passed on October 15, 2016. Before he crossed he promised he'd return yet again, and I am holding that empty space on the floor just to my right, because no one else can fill it.

Bonnie is a character made up of bits and pieces of people we have known over the years, and when you add them all together, she becomes symbolic of everything that is wrong with how the world treats animals — they are to be used and abused, then eaten or sent to auction so they can either be sold for meat or begin again at another very uncertain location. The stories our rescued friends tell me make my skin crawl, and my heart bleeds for them. But if there is one thing I've learned from them, it is that we should never give up hope, and there is always room for a miracle. So I will continue to write their stories as they inspire me, and I will follow their lead because it turns out they are far better at writing books than I will ever be.

I am deeply inspired by their courage, loyalty and love, and I hope you are, as well.

Ragano, Gertrude (buried beneath Agnes) and Mama

ANIMAL RECORD-NY SHELTER
(fill in record with pen only)

Name: Harriet   **Incoming No.** 15408

Species: Pig   **Breed:** Yorkshire/Landrace cross

Sex: female   **Age:** 1.5 years   **Incoming Date:** 07/03/08 (arrived 07/10/08)

Description/Identification Marks: Short and round pig with her back right claw missing after surgery to remove it.

History/Rescue Story: One of the pigs rescued from the Iowa floods at the end of June and beginning of July of 2008. The area where the pigs were located was near or in the town of Oakville, which is home to many pig factory farms, all of which were destroyed by the floods. Thousands of pigs died during the floods from the water but also many were shot once they reached the safety of the levees- due to fear of the levees being destroyed.

Incoming Condition: Overweight, unbelievably, with a severe infection in her back right claw. She had severe burns on the backs of her legs and ears but was in better condition than many of the pigs. *Eartag # 9607* *Yellow farm tag #217*

Personality Sweet, quiet and shy

Outgoing Information:
Date: 04/15/09 Reason: ✓ Adopted ____ Deceased If deceased: ____ Natural Death ____ Euthanasia
Injuries/illness that may have caused death:_____

Special notes about the animal's death/adoption that would be of interest to the monthly sponsor (necropsy report info on home the animal went to, etc.) _____
If adopted, name of adopter:_____ State_____

Outgoing Information recorded in the Incoming/Outgoing Animal Binder_____ Date completed_____
Record chart was faxed to Sponsorship Coordinator on _____ (date) _____ (initials) _____

ANIMAL RECORD-NY SHELTER
(fill in record with pen only)

Name: Ice

Incoming No. 17408

Species: Pig

Breed: Yorkshire/Landrace cross

Sex: gestation sow   **Age:** 1-2 years   **Incoming Date:** 6-28-08 arrived   07-01-08

Description/Identification Marks: Short + Stout, ① eye blue + right eye brown.

History/Rescue Story: One of the pigs rescued from the Iowa floods at the end of June and beginning of July of 2008. The area where the pigs were located was near or in the town of Oakville, which is home to many pig factory farms, all of which were destroyed by the floods. Thousands of pigs died during the floods from the water but also many were shot once they reached the safety of the levees- due to fear of the levees being destroyed.

Incoming Condition Covered in thick scabs on back, ears, back of legs - skin severely burnt. Possibly pregnant - pneumonia. Metal ear tag # 9606 + yellow plastic farm tag # 2430

Personality _____

Outgoing Information:
Date: 09/05/08 **Reason:** ✓ Adopted ____ Deceased If deceased: ____ Natural Death ____ Euthanasia
Injuries/illness that may have caused death: _____

Special notes about the animal's death/adoption that would be of interest to the monthly sponsor (necropsy report info info on home the animal went to, etc.) _____

If adopted, name of adopter: _____ State _____

Outgoing Information recorded in the Incoming/Outgoing Animal Binder ____ Date completed ____
Record chart was faxed to Sponsorship Coordinator on _____ (date) ____ (initials) ____

TUFTS UNIVERSITY
Hospital for Large Animals
200 Westboro Road
North Grafton, MA 01536-1895
1-508-839-7926

Document	Case Summary
Copy To:	Client
Status:	ARCHIVE

Client Information	Patient Information
	Case#: 36213
	Name: Ozzie Osbar
	Species: PORCINE **Breed:**
	Sex: BARO **DOB:** 8/11/2008
	Rvet:

Dates

Description	Date
Discharge	10/22/2009
Admission	10/22/2009

Veterinary Medical Team

Name	Title
Caitlin Vincent, DVM, Large Animal Medicine Intern	Primary Clinician
Mary Rose Paradis, DVM, MS, Diplomate ACVIM (LAIM)	Attending (Faculty) Clinician
Katherine C. Horigan, V'10	Senior Student

Diagnoses

Final diagnoses : Thoracolumbar spine subluxation
Procedures : cervical and thoracic spine radiographs
Recommendations : 1. strict stall rest for 1 month

To Our Client

Dear Schurman Family,

Client Report

On physical exam, Ozzie was bright and alert and his vitals were within normal limits. A neurology consultation confirmed that indeed Ozzie was showing neurologic signs of spasticity in his hind legs and signs that were suggestive of front limb compensation. His reflexes were tested and found to be intact which lead us to believe that the problem lies within his upper motor neuron tract (a specific pathway of his spinal cord).

Radiographs taken at Tufts today showed that Ozzie has a fracture/subluxation in the thoraco-lumbar junction of his spinal vertebrae. This fracture, most likely occurred from his traumatic fall in March, and is most likely compressing his spinal cord enough to cause these neurological signs (abnormal gait). As discussed with you, we do not recommend surgical attempts to stabilize the fracture site as the process of anesthesia and surgical preparation could result in destabilization, risking spinal cord damage, prior to surgical stabilization. The bony changes surrounding the fracture site prove that Ozzie has been attempting to stabilize this site on his own in conjunction with his powerful back muscles.

We recommend strict confined pen rest (enough room so that Ozzie can stand, sit, lie down and turn around, but not run, climb stairs, hop or step over obstacles). Please also be certain that Ozzie's enclosure has footing that keeps him from slipping. These precautions will encourage more callous (bony growth) formation to further stabilize the fractured/ subluxated vertebrae. As confirmed with our neurology department, it is unlikely that his neurological function will return to normal at the completion of his one month stall rest, but we will be happy if his neurologic status does not deteriorate further (worsening gait, uncoordinated movement, inability to rise). With good nursing care there is a good chance that Ozzie's quality of life will continue to be good.

Thank you for bringing Ozzie to Tufts! He was a wonderful patient. Please call us with any questions or concerns.

Patient Care Instructions

1) MEDICATIONS: We recommend that you discontinue giving Ozzie aspirin. As discussed it is actually a good thing for Ozzie to be aware of the pain so that he does not over-exert himself and become more active (worsen his subluxation). However, if you believe that Ozzie's pain is becoming too severe please contact us or your local veterinarian for further recommendations. We also advise that you discontinue his vitamin B injections (and any other injections) as this will also eliminate a large source of stress and movement. You may continue any oral supplementation as long as this does not stress him.

2) PHYSICAL THERAPY: Please continue passive range of motion exercises with Ozzie on his side. It will be very important to completely flex his hind legs to avoid contraction of his quadriceps muscles. You may continue to perform this when he is quiet and does not struggle.

3) CHIROPRACTIC MANIPULATION: We recommend that you discontinue the adjustments that Ozzie has been receiving in the past. It is important that Ozzie's muscles and skeletal system remains as motionless as possible to allow for further healing of the fracture site.

4) PEN REST: You report that Ozzie is currently in a 20x20 pen. We suggest that you narrow down this area in half to encourage Ozzie to remain as quiet and still as possible. As discussed, making sure that there is steady, comfortable footing and nothing for him to climb on as this will help minimize movement of his spine. Please avoid any exercise over the next month this includes going for walks, runs or rough-housing with other animals.

5) DIET: Your current diet for Ozzie seems to offer ample calcium which will continue to keep is bones strong. We do suggest that you discontinue his bran cereal as the high levels of phosphorous can actually detract from the calcium levels in his bones. You are already doing a great job at maintaining Ozzie at a good weight. Continue this program as it will decrease the amount of stress and weight that his spine will have to carry.

As always, if you have any questions or concerns regarding Ozzie please feel free to contact us. He is an amazing pig and we hope that these suggestions help him continue to do well in the future!

Follow Up Instructions

Please do not hesitate to call with any questions or concerns, (508) 839 - 5395.

Please Note

Your referring veterinarian will receive a written report regarding your animal's hospitalization.

Caitlin Vincent, DVM, Large Animal Medicine Intern

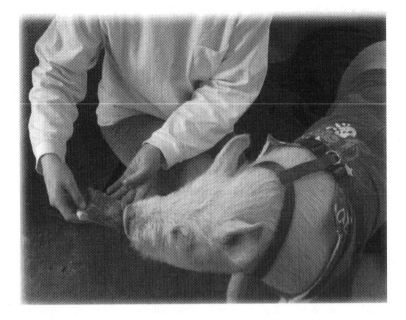

Above, Ozzie eating his favorite snack, Pizza. Below, he is at one of his Mama's book signings where Bo is watching over him like a mother lioness

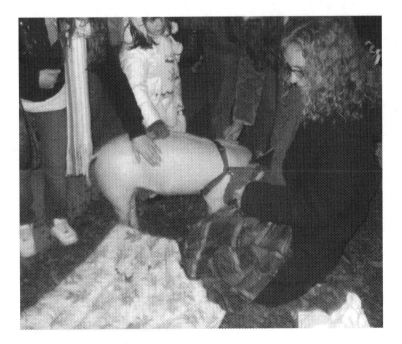

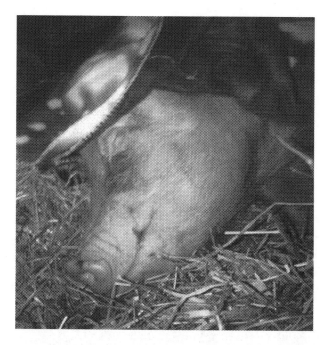

Left, Ozzie asleep under his soft fleece blankie. Below, the following summer, Iris Magnolia arrived and lived in an adjoining pen. Because of Ozzie's back and leg issues he couldn't share a hut with another pig, but he and Iris became fast friends.

OTHER BOOKS BY
KATHLEEN M. SCHURMAN

LOCKET'S MEADOW – THE LONG ROAD HOME

LOCKET'S MEADOW – CAPTAIN OF THE DANCE

OZZIE OSBOAR COUNTS TO FIFTEEN

KIDD'S KIDS

THREE DAYS IN AUGUST

Printed in the United States
By Bookmasters